Praise for Lexi Blake and Masters and Mercenaries...

"I can always trust Lexi Blake's Dominants to leave me breathless...and in love. If you want sensual, exciting BDSM wrapped in an awesome love story, then look for a Lexi Blake book."
~Cherise Sinclair USA Today Bestselling author

"Lexi Blake's MASTERS AND MERCENARIES series is beautifully written and deliciously hot. She's got a real way with both action and sex. I also love the way Blake writes her gorgeous Dom heroes--they make me want to do bad, bad things. Her heroines are intelligent and gutsy ladies whose taste for submission definitely does not make them dish rags. Can't wait for the next book!"
~Angela Knight, New York Times bestselling author

"A Dom is Forever is action packed, both in the bedroom and out. Expect agents, spies, guns, killing and lots of kink as Liam goes after the mysterious Mr. Black and finds his past and his future... The action and espionage keep this story moving along quickly while the sex and kink provides a totally different type of interest. Everything is very well balanced and flows together wonderfully."
~A Night Owl "Top Pick", Terri, Night Owl Erotica

"A Dom Is Forever is everything that is good in erotic romance. The story was fast-paced and suspenseful, the characters were flawed but made me root for them every step of the way, and the hotness factor was off the charts mostly due to a bad boy Dom with a penchant for dirty talk."
~Rho, The Romance Reviews

"A good read that kept me on my toes, guessing until the big reveal, and thinking survival skills should be a must for all men."
~Chris, Night Owl Reviews

Just One Taste

OTHER BOOKS BY LEXI BLAKE

Masters And Mercenaries
The Dom Who Loved Me
The Men With The Golden Cuffs
A Dom is Forever
On Her Master's Secret Service
Sanctum: A Masters and Mercenaries Novella
Love and Let Die
Unconditional: A Masters and Mercenaries Novella
Dungeon Royale
Dungeon Games: A Masters and Mercenaries Novella
A View to a Thrill
Cherished: A Masters and Mercenaries Novella
You Only Love Twice
Luscious: Masters and Mercenaries~Topped
Adored: A Masters and Mercenaries Novella
Master No
Just One Taste: Masters and Mercenaries~Topped 2
From Sanctum with Love, *Coming February 23, 2016*
Devoted: A Masters and Mercenaries Novella, *Coming April 12, 2106*

Masters Of Ménage (by Shayla Black and Lexi Blake)
Their Virgin Captive
Their Virgin's Secret
Their Virgin Concubine
Their Virgin Princess
Their Virgin Hostage
Their Virgin Secretary
Their Virgin Mistress

The Perfect Gentlemen (by Shayla Black and Lexi Blake)
Scandal Never Sleeps
Seduction in Session, *Coming January 5, 2016*
Big Easy Temptation, *Coming May 3, 2016*

URBAN FANTASY

Just One Taste

Masters and Mercenaries~Topped, Book 2

Lexi Blake

Just One Taste
Masters and Mercenaries, Topped, Book 2
Lexi Blake

Published by DLZ Entertainment LLC

Copyright 2015 DLZ Entertainment LLC
Edited by Chloe Vale
ISBN: 978-1-937608-48-4

McKay-Taggart logo design by Charity Hendry

Sign up for Lexi Blake's newsletter
and be entered to win a $25 gift certificate
to the bookseller of your choice.

Join us for news, fun, and exclusive content
including free short stories.

There's a new contest every month!

ACKNOWLEDGMENTS

Thanks to everyone who makes the McKay-Taggart world run. Chloe Vale, the best assistant and editor a writer could ever want—and who always gets hungry when we're working on books set in Top, my beta readers—Riane Holt and Stormy Pate. Thanks to my publicist, Danielle Sanchez—I loved working on this with you! To my friends and tireless cheerleaders, Liz Berry, Kris Cook, and Shayla Black. Special thanks to Valerie Tibbs. As always I thank my own personal Big Tag, Richard Blake. His sarcasm is always inspiring. And to the young man who formatted this book. I gave birth to him and he still charges me. I love you, Dylan. This one is for you.

CHAPTER ONE

Eric Vail stared at his boss's office. The door was closed but he knew what was going on. There was no doubt in his mind that Kyle Hawthorne was giving his stepdad the news. The question was whether Sean Taggart would think it was good news or bad news.

Maybe now wasn't the time to ask his boss for a favor.

The door to the kitchen opened and the reason for his favor breezed through. Deena Holmes. She was already dressed for work, wearing the white shirt and black slacks all the servers wore. Her dark hair was up in a neat bun, her makeup understated. She didn't need it. She was perfect the way she was. She would be perfect naked, with her hair flowing around her shoulders and no makeup on. Not that he'd seen her that way except in his dreams. And if he didn't ask for his favor, he likely never would.

She'd recently gone back to her natural brunette color. He'd liked her blonde, but she was devastating with dark hair.

"Hi, Eric," she said with a generous smile. "How are you today?"

So sweet. So polite. She'd been giving him that glowy smile for a year and for a year she'd been putting him off with polite excuses. He'd almost given up. Maybe she was simply polite and glowy to everyone. She was the girl who lit up a room and breezed through making everyone feel happy and at home. He'd almost decided she was the girl who would be kind to the grizzled-looking dude with all the scars but she would end up with the handsome lawyer.

13

Until he'd finally figured out that her handsome lawyer had turned out to be a shitbag who'd ruined her life and she needed a grizzled dude who would look out for her. He might not have some fancy degree, but he also wasn't a dirtbag who would let his wife work her ass off to put him through school and then dump her for another lawyer at his firm.

He would treat her right. He would take care of her the way she needed.

"I'm good, sweetheart. How are you?" He wanted to reach out for her and drag her into his arms and welcome her properly, but it wasn't time for that yet.

Her eyes widened at the endearment. He hadn't used it before. She recovered nicely, her smile barely faltering. "I'm great, of course. I saw the menu for tonight. Can't wait."

They all sat down for dinner after service was done. It was one of the perks of working at Top. A gourmet meal every night.

Was it the only meal she got sometimes? He'd seen the kitchen in her neat but tiny apartment. There had been very little in it. She'd needed a ride to work because her car had broken down. Had she asked him? Of course not. She'd asked Tiffany. He'd managed to work it so he'd been the one to show up on her doorstep and while she'd finished getting ready, he'd snooped.

He'd found out she either hated having groceries in her place or didn't have the money to buy them. He'd also found out that apparently in her spare time, she enjoyed doodling his name. He'd found a notebook on her dining room table with some phone numbers and jotted down information and his name with hearts.

It made him feel less like a stalker.

He wasn't. She didn't know it yet, but he was the knight in slightly tarnished armor waiting for the princess to wake up. The fact that she was doing something like doodling his name was a good sign. From what he could tell, she'd been completely shut down since her divorce. She hadn't dated, hadn't had any crazy hookups, though that wouldn't have bothered him. She could have played around with a whole football team and he wouldn't care. She deserved to have some fun after what she'd gone through. Now it looked like she was ready, but that time had closed for her. Any fun that girl was going to have now would be with him.

"I'll make sure to save you some of the brisket enchiladas. I know how much you love them." Top served elevated comfort food. The brisket enchiladas were something he'd suggested and he loved watching how much she enjoyed them.

"Thanks." Her eyes wouldn't quite meet his.

"Are you going out with the group tonight?" He knew damn well she wasn't. He kind of wanted to see if she would tell him what she was doing.

She gnawed on that full bottom lip of hers. "No. Not tonight. I've got some school stuff."

Little liar. He gave her a nod. "Hope you do well on that. Let me know if there's anything I can help you with."

Her lips curved up. "Know a lot about accounting? Because I have a test coming up and it's a killer."

"I could snipe your professor," he admitted. "That's pretty much the extent of my help in that class."

He'd been a Navy SEAL. College hadn't been in the cards for him, but when he'd gotten out, cooking school had. He'd been the only six-foot-three-inch, two hundred pounds of muscle scarred vet in a class of people ten years younger and a thousand times less damaged than him.

Deena smiled that gorgeous, world-lighting grin of hers that made his dick tighten. "I think making him your enchiladas would go over better, but I'll pass." She looked up as Tiffany walked past her. "I should go help set up. Y'all rock the kitchen tonight."

"Deena," he said as she turned toward Tiffany. He used the same voice he would have used on his men or in the kitchen when he wanted to get someone's attention, though he would admit he tried to add a silky edge that was only for her. He'd turned his military leader voice into his Dom voice.

It worked. She stopped in her tracks and turned back around, giving him her full attention. "Yes?"

"If that jerk comes back in, I want to know." He gave her what he hoped was a stern glare so she understood this wasn't a request. Though he technically wasn't her boss, he was the number two at Top and he took the safety of everyone at the place seriously.

She flushed and rolled her eyes. "That was nothing."

A customer had put his hand on her ass, causing her to drop a whole platter of drinks. He'd claimed it had all been an accident, but the guy was a regular and he always sat in Deena's section and he always was alone. Yeah, he tried to keep an eye on that guy.

Tiffany shook her head as she stopped. "That guy's weird and he's totally got a thing for her. Not that having a thing for her is weird, but from that jerk, it is."

Tiffany was infinitely more reasonable than Deena. He turned his attention to her. "Let whoever is the hostess tonight know that Deena's section is full and will be all evening."

"That isn't necessary," Deena said, her eyes widening.

"Will do." Tiffany gave him a jaunty salute and a wink. "I'll make sure that ass feels right at home."

Tiffany turned and walked toward the front.

Deena shook her head. "I can handle Jerry."

He cocked a brow. "I'm sure you can, but you don't have to. I'm serious, sweetheart. I do not want to hear about you putting yourself in danger over a tip."

"Fine. But only because he's a shitty tipper." She ran off behind her friend.

She could run but after tonight, he wasn't letting her hide anymore. He would have watched over her, waiting until the time was right, but thank god she'd moved the damn clock up. He was dying. He couldn't date because he didn't want anyone other than her. And he was too old to hook up with women for sex.

He wanted more and he wanted it with Deena.

The door came open and Sean walked out first, Kyle second. Kyle stopped and shook his stepfather's hand, his jaw squared.

Taggart nodded and said something to Kyle before Kyle turned.

Sean glanced around and then gestured for Eric to join him. His boss had a stern look on his face and Eric winced inwardly. Sean Taggart had been a Green Beret, but the man would have made a damn fine drill sergeant. Eric had to wonder if he was about to get a dressing down. He strode forward because he preferred to get the bad shit over as quickly as possible.

What the hell was he going to do if Sean wouldn't help him?

Could he go through with tonight's class knowing he might have to watch the woman of his dreams with another man?

He walked into Sean's office and waited for his boss to take a seat before settling himself into the big chair across from the desk.

Sean stared at him, those blue eyes of his steady in a way that would likely make most men look away.

Eric had been stared down by the best. He simply waited. Patience in all things. It was a motto of his.

"Do you know what my stepson just told me?"

Yes. He definitely knew the answer to that question. "Not the exact words, of course, but I suspect he informed you that he signed his enlistment papers yesterday."

Sean sat back. "What gave you the right to talk him into joining the Navy, Eric?"

Damn. He hated disappointing his boss. Sean had given him a job when no one else wanted an almost forty-year-old, just-out-of-school chef who looked more like a mobster than a man who could cook. Sean had moved him quickly to the role of sous chef, training Eric in his own techniques and being one of the most sincerely helpful men Eric had ever met. Still, he wasn't ashamed of what he'd done. Kyle had worked at Top for several months and they'd become friendly. "He asked my opinion. I gave it."

Sean shook his head and then groaned. "If only I could explain it to my wife in such simple terms. She's going to flip out."

Eric softened a bit. "He needs it. He's got no idea what he wants to do with his life. It certainly isn't working in a kitchen."

Sean's eyes closed briefly. "I know. I also know he showed up drunk two weeks ago and you covered for him."

Not a lot got past the boss. "I didn't think that was something his mother should see. She was coming in for dinner that night."

"Were there episodes I didn't know about?"

He wasn't going to lie to the man. He might be willing to cover for the kid, but not directly lie to Sean. "Yes. He's struggling with something though he didn't want to talk about it."

"His best friend from childhood died last year. He's been out of control ever since," Sean explained. "He dropped out of grad school and we've been trying to help him find his way. He's been drinking.

I'm worried he'll slide into something worse. I believe the military could help him in this case. He's undisciplined, unfocused. Thank god you said it because Grace really had a problem when I brought it up."

"Not that we should tell her I said it." Grace could be formidable all on her own.

Sean chuckled. "Oh, this was all your idea, buddy." He sobered. "Seriously, thank you for being kind to him. I'm very glad he signed those papers before telling his mother."

"It's a sign that he's ready. He didn't want her to talk him out of it." Having spent time with the kid he knew Kyle wasn't bad, he was struggling and now he had a plan to get his life back on track. "If it helps Grace any, I don't believe he'll make a career of it. I think he'll eventually want to go back to school. It's something he needs right now. He needs to feel like his life has purpose."

"I agree with you, and you're going to need a stiff drink after my wife finds out you're the one who convinced her baby boy to join the Navy. Grace has certain fears when it comes to losing her loved ones. Not that we don't all have them, but she went through the death of her first husband so she's more sensitive than a lot of people. She doesn't always understand that the risk is worth the reward. See, I've been coming up with all this stuff to tell her because I was dreading the moment I had to take a stand. Now I don't have to." Sean seemed to be warming to the idea. "I can honestly say I had nothing to do with it, but of course I support the decision since we can't get him out of it now. It's the best of both worlds for me."

Thank god. He saw his in. "You know, boss, I was hoping you could do me a favor."

"Absolutely. What do you need?"

This was one of the things he admired about his boss. Sean simply said yes without being told what he needed. Of course Sean was also very careful about the people he hired and let into his small circle. He wouldn't bring anyone in he didn't trust. Though they were roughly the same age, he looked up to Sean as a mentor in not only business but life. "I need you to talk to your brother."

Sean's face went tight for a moment. "Which one?"

Eric wished he hadn't phrased it like that. Saying "brother" likely reminded Sean that he'd recently lost one. Theo Taggart had died on a mission for the firm the oldest Taggart brother ran, and no one had recovered from it. They might never recover. "I'm sorry. I meant Ian. I need you to ask Ian for a favor tonight. I'm in the training class at Sanctum."

"Yes, I recommended you for the program. I promise I'll get you out of here early so you can be on time." Sean gave him a pointed look. "You should be on time. Ian does mean shit to Doms who show up late. His sister-in-law calls him Satan and she's not that far off. Unless you're Macon, and I swear Macon could punch my brother in the face and as long as he gave him a pie afterward, all would be forgiven. Huh. I wonder if I could get away with throwing one of Macon's pies in his face. He'd be so distracted by the taste, I would have a serious head start."

"I'll be on time," Eric promised. "But I understand that partners are assigned on the first night of training."

Sean's eyes narrowed. "You want me to make sure you get assigned to Deena."

He was fairly certain his skin was a nice shade of red. What that woman could make him do. "Yes. I was hoping you could convince him to do that for me."

"Is that such a great idea? You two work together."

"We work in the same space. She's not in the kitchen and not under my direction. Besides, Ally and Macon are married."

"Yes, but he's the pie maker," Sean pointed out. "Even if I wanted to fire one of them, I would have to go through Ian. He still owns half this place until I make enough to buy him out."

Was he serious? For the first time Eric got a bit unsettled. He hadn't thought that Sean would have a problem with him dating Deena.

"Eric, have you thought this through?" Sean asked quietly. "From what I understand she's not exactly chasing after you or anyone for that matter. Don't get me wrong. She's a lovely woman, but she shuts down when it comes to intimacy."

"That's not true. She's quite comfortable with intimacy." It was one of the reasons he thought she was ready. "Not physically, but emotionally. She's the one everyone goes to with their problems. She's the one who listens."

Sean shook his head. "That's not true intimacy. She listens but she never talks. I wouldn't know she was divorced if I hadn't run a check on her." His eyes narrowed. "How did you find out? Or did she tell you?"

Eric shrugged. "I might have run my own check. And she does get chatty when she has a couple of glasses of wine. I stay fairly close to the women when we all go out."

He was sure he looked ridiculous, like a large predatory bulldog watching over the pretty butterflies, but some of the clubs they went to could be dangerous. He'd caught an asshole slipping something into Deena's drink once.

The man likely wouldn't do it again. Luckily, she hadn't been watching and his friend Javier had changed the drink and kept her occupied while Eric dealt with the situation.

"For which I'm eternally grateful. Are you doing the same thing here? Are you trying to watch over her?"

Again, he couldn't lie to Sean. "I'm trying to keep every other man in the world off her so I can have her for myself."

Sean sighed. "I wish I could help you, but the training partners have already been selected. Ian is very strict about the pairing process. He and Kai Ferguson spent hours selecting the proper partner for each trainee and I don't think he's going to be swayed."

So he'd hit a wall here. When he couldn't go through a wall, he went around it. "Thank you, sir. I'll contact Ian on my own."

Sean rolled his eyes. "God save me from freaking upstanding SEALs. You've already got Deena. I would have made sure of it, but Kai put you two together, which means he thinks you're a good match. Actually, so do I. I think she needs someone like you in her life. She needs someone who can be patient with her. I was worried when I found out she'd taken the Sanctum offer."

"She's curious. I think she believes she's going to go out there and sow some wild oats, but she'll end up getting hurt."

"She's not the kind of woman who can have a string of one-night stands and come out of it whole," Sean agreed. "She's a one-man woman who happened to get the wrong man and now she's determined to change. It could go seriously wrong."

"I don't intend to allow that to happen." He had plans and being

Deena's Dom was the perfect way to set them in motion. Patience. In his SEAL team, he'd been the best sniper because he could sit motionless for hours at a time. One assignment he'd stayed in his perch for a week before taking out his target. He'd smelled like hell at the end and sometimes he was sure his spine had been permanently messed up, but he'd gotten the job done.

He would get this one done too. After all, this was the most important mission of his life. This was the rest of his life. He'd served his country and now he wanted his prize. Her.

Sean stood and held out his hand. "I'm glad to hear it. But whatever you do don't tell my brother you intend to steal that girl. This whole program is about bringing in singles because everyone is pairing off and he's got Doms who need subs to play with. So don't mention the whole 'you're in love with her' thing."

Eric felt a grin slide across his face as he shook his boss's hand. He wouldn't admit it, but getting Sean's approval was important to him. He would still have gone after Deena, but he was damn happy to know he had Sean's blessing. "Not only will I not tell Big Tag, I think I'll keep it from Deena for a while."

"You know, I would have thought you would fight the whole love thing."

Not at all. He hadn't even thought about fighting it. When he'd seen her, gotten close to her, he'd known she was the one. "I'm not a stupid man. I've seen some bad shit. I know a good thing when it comes along and I've learned that good things are worth fighting for."

And tonight, he started the real fight of his life.

* * * *

"What is up with Eric? He's in a weird mood tonight." Deena locked her purse up and turned to Tiffany, hoping and praying that her friend couldn't tell that she felt all flushed and anxious because merely being in the same room with that man was enough to get her hormones flowing. Yes, being near the man did that to her and then he'd gone and called her sweetheart in that deep as night voice of his. She'd damn near had an orgasm right there.

Could the sound of a man's voice cause her womb to spasm? It seemed to.

Tiffany looked in the mirror of the employee lounge and smoothed down her hair. Her hands had small flecks of paint still on them, as though she'd gotten up from her easel to come to work, which she very likely had done. She was an artist and she painted every chance she got. "I don't know if you've noticed but Eric is a tiny bit protective."

She leaned against the locker and tried not to think about how hot he'd looked. Or how he'd made her feel when he'd called her sweetheart. "I suppose, though he should stick to the kitchen. He doesn't understand what goes on in the front of house. He should keep his nose out of it."

His gorgeous, masculine nose that went so well with his face and his ridiculously large body.

She had to remind herself of all the reasons she wasn't getting involved with him. A—She wasn't getting involved with anyone. She was so over involvement. B—He was too much. Too gorgeous. Too masculine. Too sexy. She couldn't keep Eddie around. There was no way she would be able to satisfy a man like Eric Vail. C—She didn't play where she worked.

She pretty much didn't play at all, but now that she was going to, it wouldn't be with a man she had to work with. Especially not the sous chef. If it came down to a choice, there was zero question who would win. Servers were easy to find. Eric's brisket was not.

Tiffany's eyes widened. "I wouldn't say that around the man if I were you. You know you're going to have to watch that if you're going to survive the training program."

A little thrill went through her. It all started tonight. "Watch what? And I think I can handle the training program. I'm looking forward to it."

She'd been counting the days since she'd been accepted. When Grace Taggart had explained that Sanctum was taking new trainees and they would allow Top employees to train in exchange for later work at the club, she'd jumped at the chance. Sanctum was the single most exclusive club in Texas. It wasn't something she could ever afford and now all she had to do was wait tables once a week and she got a membership? Count her in.

Maybe, just maybe, she could find an outlet, have some fun. Maybe she could find a lover. Oh, not a lover as in she would love him. She was totally done with that. But someone she could try sex with. Put her toe back in that deep, scary pond she'd nearly drowned in.

"The first time you turn that mouth on your training Dom, you're going to get a real not erotic spanking," Tiffany said with a shake of her head.

Tiffany was going in with her. She was so happy to not do this alone. She gave her friend a saucy grin. "You are absolutely as untrained as me so you don't know."

Tiffany chuckled. "Yes, well I've read way more romance novels than you have. In Amber Rose's books the Doms always get spanky when the subs talk smack. And from what I've heard, those Doms are based on the Sanctum Doms, so you should watch out." She sobered a bit. "And you can't talk that way around any of them. Not when it comes to work. It won't matter that Chef has nothing to do with the training program. It will get back to him that you're the brat of the class, and how is that going to make you feel?"

She hadn't even thought about that, but it didn't matter. "I'm going to behave perfectly. I'm not going into this on a whim. I want to explore and find myself, and this is a safe way to do it. I'm only being mouthy because Eric is going to cost me money."

"Who's being mouthy about what?" Ally strode through the door, ready for work. She had a smile on her lips and damn it, but the girl glowed a bit. There was no question what put the sunny expression on that girl's face.

Sex. Sex with a superhot ex-soldier who adored her. Ally was married to Macon Miles, the pastry chef who apparently could do way more for a girl than ice a cupcake.

Tiffany pointed Deena's way. "That one about you know who."

Ally opened her locker and slid her bag inside. "What did Eric do? Did he finally ask her out for real?"

"He's never asked me out and that's a good thing because I would be forced to turn him down." For all of her alphabetical reasons.

But mostly because he scared the holy hell out of her.

"He's totally asked you out," Tiffany replied. "He's just sneaky about it."

She shook her head because she wasn't sure what she would do with an Eric who was actively pursuing her. And she couldn't remember a single time he'd asked out. "No. He's never wanted to date me."

Ally shook her head. "That's so sad. I thought I was unaware. You take the cake, D."

What were they talking about? "I'm rarely alone with the man and honestly he doesn't pay that much attention to me."

The one time she'd been alone with him, she'd nearly fallen all over herself trying to get ready because he'd shown up twenty minutes early to pick her up for work. She'd been expecting Tiffany, but she'd opened the door and her tongue had nearly rolled out of her mouth because he'd stood there looking so lickable it hurt.

She'd rushed to get ready because the last thing she wanted was for Eric to truly understand how pitifully she lived. He would see her threadbare furniture and how crappy her décor was. He would likely wonder what the hell she did with her money, and she wasn't about to admit she was still paying off debt from her first marriage.

Luckily, Eric Vail was practically Captain America. He was all moral and upstanding and would never stoop to spy on a fellow employee so she'd been safe. When she'd rushed out of her bedroom, he'd been standing by the door. He probably hadn't moved the whole time.

He wasn't a bad boy and she was going out to find herself one. A bad boy couldn't break her heart. A bad boy might be able to make her feel like a woman. Even if it was only for an hour or two. That was all she needed from a man, all she would accept.

"You know all those times he's asked if you have anything to do this weekend and do you want to hang out at his place? Or hey, a bunch of the gang's going to see a movie. Why don't you come?"

"He's only being nice." He was a sincerely nice man. He cared about his coworkers. He watched out for them. Sometimes he beat the shit out of people. He thought she hadn't known what he was doing to the dirtbag who'd tried to roofie her drink. He'd even told her that he was only holding the guy until the police came, but she wasn't an idiot. That dude had not gotten a black eye by himself.

But he would have done that for anyone. Right?

Ally laughed. "He's not being nice. Don't get me wrong, I like Eric, but I don't know that I would call the man nice. It's his way of getting close to you. You won't let him in any other way. He actually asked you out once. He asked you if you were free on Monday about two weeks after you hired on."

She remembered the day. She'd smiled and told him that she had classes on Mondays. "Oh, no. He was asking me because everyone was putting in an extra shift to get the new tables in."

Ally groaned. "She's extremely good at rewriting history. No. He asked if you wanted to grab something to eat. He didn't work that day."

Had she misinterpreted him so badly? Had Captain America asked her out? She shivered at the thought and about half of it was from fear. "No. I can't go out with him."

Tiffany shot her an incredulous look. "Why? He's a stand-up guy."

Because she wanted him. Because she dreamed about him at night. Because she no longer trusted her own instincts. "I'm not attracted to him."

"So you stare at him because you're not attracted to him?" Ally asked. "Because most of us like to look at the guys we're attracted to."

Why wouldn't they let this be? "I don't stare at him." She did it all the time. She would catch a glimpse of the man and not be able to look away. She would walk into the kitchen and he would be stirring something or working over the hot stove and she would stand there for a minute before remembering what she'd come in to do. "Or if I do, it's me zoning out and he happens to be standing there. I wouldn't be surprised if he moved into my line of sight just so everyone will think I'm staring at him."

Tiffany looked over at Ally, her mouth open. "Is she serious?"

"She's ridiculous and she's scared out of her mind and I have to wonder how she got past the shrink." Ally frowned. "You didn't lie to Kai, did you? Because he's an avowed sadist and that could go poorly for you."

She wasn't sure she was ready for a sadist, but a baby Dom would do. "I was honest with him. I told him what I want. I want to explore my own sexuality and see if this lifestyle can help me find some of the things I need. Like self-confidence."

Tiffany wrapped her up in a hug. "I think it will, sweetie. I think it might help both of us."

"Self-confidence?" Ally seemed confused. "You have a ton of confidence."

Ally hadn't known her as long as Tiffany. "I am very good at faking it."

"The divorce took a lot more than cash from Deena," Tiffany said, squeezing her again before going back to fixing her hair. "It took her confidence in herself and men."

"I've never had confidence in men," Deena admitted. A faithless father had taken that long before her ex-husband had done his damage.

Ally sat down on the small couch and sighed. "Well, maybe the training program will do more for you than you think because a good Dom can restore your faith in men. Have either one of you heard who you've been partnered with? You probably won't know their names but Macon might."

"Does Macon know who's in the program with us?" Deena was certainly curious.

Ally shook her head. "It's all very confidential. Only the Taggarts know who they invited. You and Tiffany probably aren't supposed to talk about it."

"We're only talking about it with each other and you," Tiffany argued. "I hope we don't have to share. I heard there's an extreme lack of single Doms."

"It's kind of both ways," Ally explained. "The way I hear it, there are some powerful members without subs to play with and the subs who are willing to play want more choices. It all makes Big Tag irritable and then he needs a pie. I swear Macon is like his bartender except with sweets."

"Where does he put it all?" Tiffany asked. "Because there isn't an ounce of fat on that man. I'm happy to go to Sanctum to watch that man in a pair of leathers. Not that I would do more than watch

26

because his wife is super scary. I want to be her when I grow up."

"Everyone wants to be her," Ally agreed. "And I don't think you're going to share baby Doms. I overheard Kai talking to Big Tag about how happy he is with the partnership selection process. I've heard a rumor that Kai thinks at least one of the pairs is a perfect match. And don't tell anyone I said that because my husband will take a spatula to my butt. What happens at Sanctum is supposed to stay at Sanctum."

She wished that perfect match well because she intended to play. "I'm looking forward to tonight and the coming weeks. I hope my baby Dom is a seriously bad boy. I want him hot and nasty because I intend to have sex with him."

She was going to figure out why Ally glowed when she walked into a room. Why Grace Taggart lit up when she saw her husband. She wanted to know why a woman truly chased after a man.

She'd kind of fallen in with Eddie. She couldn't say it was a mad love story. She'd started high school and met Eddie and five years later she'd married him because she'd had nothing better to do. It had seemed like it was time.

She wanted to know what it felt like to lust after a guy. What it felt like to truly want someone.

Ally stared her way. "You think that's a good idea? You might not like him."

Whoever he was he would be Kai Ferguson approved, and that gave her some confidence. Kai was smart and cared about the people he counseled. He wouldn't put her with someone she wasn't compatible with. "I'll like him."

"Like you like Eric?" Tiffany asked.

She was pretty sure she turned beet red. "I don't. I mean I like him because he's nice, but I don't like like him."

She totally like liked him. She simply wasn't going to act on her like liking.

"I have to ask you why." Ally moved forward, her eyes steady on Deena. "Eric is amazing. I know he's a little scary, but he's also wonderful."

She caught on the part she could use. "He can be scary when he wants to be."

The door opened again and Jenni bounced in. "Oooo, are we talking about Eric? He's totally scary. The other day I very innocently mentioned that his mole sauce needed salt and I'd put some in for him and I nearly peed my pants when he looked at me."

Deena's jaw dropped. "You're lucky you didn't get your ass fired. You don't screw with a chef's sauce."

Jenni shrugged. "Chef yelled at me for a long time and I cried and then everything was all right. And it needed salt."

Now there was a girl who would get her ass spanked if she ever tried to take a training class. "Yeah, well, he should be scary when you do that."

"Oh, he's kind of always scary," Jenni said. "The scar freaks me out. That is one ugly dude."

She got in the twenty-year-old, never had a real problem in the world until Daddy made her get a job's face. "Don't you dare call him that, you shallow bitch."

Jenni's eyes were huge in her face and she took a step back. "Okay, now you're scary. I'm going to go and set up for dinner."

She rushed back out.

"Hey, we all know Jenni's got issues. There's no need to start a fight," Tiffany said, her voice calm.

"She's a mean girl and I don't like mean girls." She couldn't stand bullies.

"Don't be so hard on her. She's young and this is her first real experience outside a prep school." Ally frowned and looked over at the door.

"I can make it her last." She had no right to call Eric ugly. It was false in the first place. That scar made him heroic, manly. There was nothing wrong with that man's face. Absolutely nothing.

"Please don't." Ally put a hand on her shoulder. "She's the daughter of one of Ian Taggart's biggest clients. He got her the job and she's usually all right at it. Since they moved her to the hostess station, she's been okay."

"She spends all her time flirting."

"She's also excellent at table management and she's good at making sure we all get customers," Tiffany said with finality. "That girl can smell a good tipper from a mile away and she spreads out the wealth. It's a thing that brings harmony to all of us, so let's ignore the fact that she's not interested in your honey."

"He's not my honey." After tonight she wouldn't have to worry about it. "And he's not interested in me. We're friends and coworkers."

And that was the way it was going to stay.

CHAPTER TWO

Eric watched her as she moved out onto the main stage. Deena walked in with the other subs, two women he didn't know and Tiffany. Work was about to get very interesting. He wasn't sure what Deena and Tiffany would do when they realized he and Javier were here, too.

His lips had started to curl up when he realized she wasn't dressed like the other women. Tiffany and the two others were in full fet wear, complete with beautiful corsets, frilly thongs or boy shorts, and stunning heels. Deena had on a leather miniskirt and a tight tank top that had likely come straight from the same place her everyday clothes came from. Her feet were bare, making her inches shorter than the rest of the girls. She smiled, but when she thought no one was looking, she would smooth out her clothes as though attempting to make up for their lack of flair.

"Those are some fine women." Javier stepped up next to him. Like Eric, he was wearing leathers—pants and a vest, no shirt. Javi had cowboy boots on while Eric preferred the combat boots he'd worn for years. You can take the SEAL out of the Navy, but try to take his fucking boots and he would shoot you. That was his motto anyway.

"They certainly are." Though she was dressed more modestly than the other women, she was the one who held his attention. Her hair was pulled back in a sweet braid that was simply going to have to go. He wanted to see her with her hair around her shoulders, her head bent and waiting for his command.

Damn, he was already hard. He started naming all the ingredients he would need for tomorrow night's Provençal chicken dish. Chicken thighs, kosher salt, cracked black pepper…

"Are you doing that thing where you prepare a dish in your head so your dick will go down?" Javi asked.

"Yes." There was no point in denying it. Herbes de Provence. Flour. Lemon.

"You know most of us think about baseball," Javi pointed out. "Damn, Tiffany's got a fine ass on her. If I didn't think of that like a sister, I would be praying she's my partner." Javi stopped. "Shit, what if she's my partner? I don't think I can spank her."

"That was all up to the big guy and Kai." He seemed to have his dick under control for the moment. "It's only six weeks."

Six weeks where they would practice and train and be partners. Six weeks where Deena would be forced to lean on him and he could prove to her that he could take care of her.

Damn. There it went again. She was talking to a tall, severe-looking woman who couldn't possibly be a sub and Deena's eyes lit up.

"Come on," Javi said. "We're wanted on the stage."

It was time. He hoped she didn't run the minute she saw him. The other two men he'd met earlier in the locker room moved by him. Gage Jensen was an ER doc and Harrison Keen was one of Dallas's top-rated criminal attorneys.

So who was the obvious baby Domme for? That was interesting. Eric was looking forward to the evening. He walked with Javi to the main stage.

Stage was just a name, but it could be meaningful on certain nights. Tonight was not one of those nights. Tonight was merely a training night.

His first training night.

Despite the fact that he'd been in more clubs than he could name, he'd never had formal training and that meant he was a baby Dom at Sanctum.

Alex McKay and Liam O'Donnell were out on the main stage, talking amongst themselves. Alex had a clipboard in his hand and was

31

pointing out things to his partner. Both Masters were large men, overpowering and obviously dominant. Both men were also married. Their wives, Eve and Avery, would be mentoring the submissives.

He saw the moment she realized he was here. Deena's eyes widened and she walked over and started whispering to Tiffany, who immediately looked over and her jaw dropped.

Had they thought they were the only ones who had been invited?

"What the hell are you doing here?" Deena asked, her voice rising.

Alex stepped in front of her. Eric couldn't see his expression but both women immediately looked down, heads bowed. "Lesson number one. Politeness is required at Sanctum. I expect it from everyone. Not only subs. If a Dom in this club is rude to another member, I will deal with it. If a sub is rude, then his or her dominant partner will deal with it."

Deena brought her head up. "I'm sorry, Sir. I was surprised to see a coworker here. I don't know that's the best idea. Eric and Javier work with Tiffany and me at Top. It could make things awkward at work."

Eric stared at her, not giving her a second's sympathy. Javi joined him, standing at his side. Fuck. What if she convinced the instructors to separate them? He'd expected her to be surprised. He hadn't expected she would make a scene.

Liam O'Donnell chuckled. "If we didn't accept coworkers, we wouldn't have a damn club and most of us wouldn't be married."

McKay seemed way less amused by the situation. "If you think it's going to be awkward, then you should leave because the offer of training was given to all the Top employees, not simply you and your friend. If Eric and Javier are here it's because they have needs. Should your needs come before theirs? I think if it's going to be awkward at work, it's because you'll make it awkward. Lesson number two. Being a sub is all about making choices. You choose to submit. You choose what you're willing to accept and what you won't. So this is your first choice, Deena. Are you going to stay or go? Please understand if you stay, you'll get the first spanking of the training class. You signed a contract that stated you would be polite at all times and treat your fellow trainees with respect. You broke that

within two minutes of stepping out of the locker room. We'll begin
with a count of twenty from your training Dom, and no you do not get
a choice in who that person will be. He was selected carefully and
with mind to true compatibility. You'll accept him and his discipline
or walk away now."

Did Alex have to be so harsh with her?

Deena's head came up and there was no doubt in her eyes. "I'll
accept him and the discipline, Sir. I'm very sorry for my rudeness.
No, I don't believe my needs come before theirs and I wish Eric and
Javi every bit of joy they can find. I know that's why I'm here and I
promise to honor my contract from now on."

"Then we're pleased to have you." Alex turned back to Eric.
"Master Eric, you owe your submissive some discipline."

He was going to need way more than his next recipe to get
through this. He prayed Deena didn't notice the massive hard-on he
suddenly had.

His night was looking up.

* * * *

Yep. That was how her night was going.

"Are you really going to do this?" Tiffany whispered. "Are you
going to let the sous chef braise your backside?"

The sous chef looked like sin on two legs. She thought the man
was hot in chef's whites. He was devastating in leathers. Tall and
broad and muscular. He had those notches at his hips that made
women lose their flipping minds. The leather pants rode low,
exposing his six-pack and a whole bunch of bronze skin she kind of
wanted to lick. She could push back that vest he was wearing and put
her hands all over him.

He was going to spank her. Her hands were shaking at the
thought, and not in fear.

"I don't have much of a choice if I want to stay." She looked over
and Master Liam was talking quietly with Eric. Master Eric, though
for now the term was simply honorary. He wouldn't have full Master
rights at Sanctum until he'd completed the training program to the
satisfaction of Master Ian. It was far tougher for a Dom to gain access

33

to the club than a submissive.

Eric was her Dom for the next six weeks. She was fairly certain that was a terrible idea, but there was nothing she could do about it tonight. She'd screwed up enough for her first five minutes as a sub.

"You should be glad you're not my sub, sweetheart." Althea stood over her. Althea Walsh had a good half a foot on her. The newbie Domme had been laughing and smiling in the locker room even as she'd changed into her latex cat suit with heels Deena was certain she wouldn't be able to even stand in. The minute they'd walked out of the locker room, she'd become a different human being entirely. An icy calm had come over Althea and her eyes had sharpened like a predator scenting prey.

Deena totally agreed with that assessment. "Me, too. I think you're probably rough on a girl."

Althea's eyes went to the other side of the stage. "Honey, I'm not anything on a girl. Give me a man to top."

"Well, it won't be Eric," she heard herself saying.

Althea's brow rose. "You're aching for some discipline, sweetheart."

"Or she got jealous at the thought of you touching her Dom." Tiffany was grinning like this was the best entertainment she'd ever seen.

"I was not," she shot back.

Althea's perfectly made up lips curled. "Oh, this is going to be fun. I think I'll make sure I get a seat."

Master Liam seemed to be finished imparting whatever wisdom he had about beating her butt and Eric stepped back. He was perfectly calm and she was fairly certain her face was as red as her backside was likely to be. He walked over to Javier and started speaking to him as though nothing out of the ordinary was happening.

Why the hell was he here? She knew that was the very question that had gotten her into trouble, but she so wanted to know the answer. Eric Vail wasn't supposed to want to spank a girl's ass. He was supposed to be the guy who would be shocked at the thought of even harming a hair on a woman's head. She would never in a million years have pegged him as a man interested in the D/s lifestyle.

Damn he looked good in leathers.

"I can't believe he's here." Tiffany stepped up with her, watching the other side of the room. "Javi, I can see. He's a total pervert, but Eric is so…noble."

Yep. He sure was. "I have no idea. And apparently we're some kind of match, which I don't see at all. I don't think there's anything I can do about it tonight."

Tomorrow was an entirely different thing. Tomorrow she could sort everything out. She would still have to be in the same class and deal with all the issues that would arise from that, but she wouldn't have a coworker as her Dom.

For one night only, maybe she could indulge in a fantasy.

"All right, let's pair up and then get this class going," Liam said, quickly calling out names and pairing people up. Javier ended up with the blonde named Mia. Althea was partnered with someone named Harrison. Unlike the Doms, he wore no vest, his cut chest on display. He had curly ebony-colored hair and piercing emerald eyes that turned down the minute Althea stood in front of him. Tiffany was paired up with a lean man with short golden hair and a ready smile. He shook her hand as he introduced himself as Gage.

Eric stood at the far side of the stage, staring at her. He made no move to come to her.

Maybe he was more of a Dom than she gave him credit for. She was going to have to smooth some things over with him. It wasn't like he would really spank her. She expected he would lightly tap her backside and she would make some little crying noises. It was all in fun after all.

There was nothing to do but brazen through it so she started to make her way to him. She would give herself over to the experience and she and Eric would be able to laugh about it later. He couldn't be any happier than she was because despite what they had talked about earlier, she was certain he wasn't lusting after her. He was likely as horrified to see her here as she was him.

"I'm sorry." She gave him what she hoped was an apologetic smile. "I got us in trouble on the first day."

His eyes pinned her. Those dark orbs were radiating authority in a way she'd never seen from him before. It reminded her that he hadn't always been a chef. Once he'd led men into dangerous situations. "You got yourself in trouble, Deena. The next time it happens, I'll be the one setting the punishment and it will be harsh. Your behavior reflects on me. Try to remember that."

Wow, he was good with the icy cold commands. "I will remember that. So you have to spank me now. Should we talk about that?"

"We don't have to talk about it. Was it in your contract that you would allow spanking? You should have signed a rudimentary contract with simple answers about initial play. We'll go over a much more detailed contract tomorrow night."

When they would sign the contract that would bind them together for the next six weeks. The thought sent a shiver down her spine. And she had signed that initial contract. Her first spanking. She'd never tried it before. She read about it in books and thought about what it would feel like. Her whole life was nothing but work and study. The days had become endless. She'd worked two jobs after her divorce to pay for the mountain of debt her ex had piled up. She was finally free and clear. She was about to graduate. It was time to move on. It was time to find out if this lifestyle that called to her was truly right.

Was she going to turn away because the man giving her this first experience wasn't perfect? Or rather was far too perfect?

"Deena?" His voice had softened slightly. He was standing over her. "Are you going to submit or not?"

It probably wouldn't even be that good. After all, superheroes didn't typically spank bad girls. This was her element. He would likely discover it wasn't his. She was safe enough. She tilted her chin up to look him in the eye. "Do your worst, Vail."

His hand came up, catching her hair and drawing her head back. "That's Master Eric or Sir to you. Don't make this worse than it has to be. I'll expect submission for the rest of the evening. Let's not look like the bickering couple everyone loves to hate. There's always one in any group. I would rather it not be us." He leaned in and she could almost swear he was smelling her hair. It should have creeped her out, but she found it ridiculously sexy that Eric Vail was running his nose over her neck and up to her ear. "This can be easy between us or it can be hard. It's all your choice, sweetheart."

Her skin was already tingling. "I'm ready."

His words were hot against her ear. "I doubt that very much."

He released her and when she looked over, Tiffany was staring openly at them. Most of the group had been watching her and Eric. He was right. They were already the problem children of the group. She was screwing up and she wasn't going to do it again. She wasn't going to embarrass Eric again.

She could do this.

"I believe we're ready for the impromptu show," Master Alex said. He took a seat in one of the folding chairs they'd set up for the class.

Before she could take another breath, they had an audience.

She was not going to be self-conscious. Nope. No way. This was all part of the lifestyle. Quite frankly, the idea of being watched was tempting. She could get her toe wet with a very staid, over-the-clothes spanking. She would get it over with and see that she could handle Eric. It was nothing more than a classmate relationship.

Eric pulled up a chair and sat himself down. Even sitting he looked like a strong soldier, the type of man other men followed. The type of man women who were looking for an upstanding man would melt over. Not that she was doing it or anything.

She gave him a bright smile to try to make him feel more comfortable. He was likely feeling weird about spanking her. "Let's get this over with. I do promise I'm going to be sweet as pie from now on."

"Some of my favorite pies are spicy, sweetheart, so don't think you always have to be sweet. Do you want to pull the skirt up or down?"

So he wanted to get a little saucy. Good thing she had on a pretty pair of panties. "Pull it up. Sorry. Hope you're not embarrassed."

His lips turned up in the sexiest grin and his eyes heated in a way that made her breath catch. "I'm not embarrassed, sweetheart. But I am eager to get through this. When we're done, you will sit in my lap, as you will for the rest of the class. There is no chair for you. There is only my lap. Am I understood?"

Whoa. He had the Dom thing down. No doubt about that. He'd deepened his voice and his eyes were steady on her. She found herself nodding and unable to stop herself from moving toward him. He was waiting for an answer. She tried to remember the question. Understood? Did she understand? Nope. Not at all. She'd dreamed about this day for over a year and the last thing she'd expected would happen was being told by her work crush that she wasn't allowed to sit anywhere except his lap. "I understand."

She could handle all of this. She was strong and brave and she could handle a spanking and sitting on a guy's lap. That was the whole point of this exercise. She was in control. It would all be fine.

When he patted his lap, she made the decision that she wasn't going to drag it out. She was going to prove to all of them that she could hack this lifestyle. She moved with what she hoped was some grace and placed herself over his lap. She squirmed as she tried to find a comfortable place. She nearly gasped when she felt him pull at what little material made up her skirt. He was looking at her backside, at her silky black undies. At least they were the nice ones.

"Oh, this won't do," he said as she felt his fingers slide under the band of her bikini panties. "Here's another rule. None of these. No panties. Tonight I'll give them back to you at the end of the session, but if I catch you with them again, I'll cut them off you. Is that understood?"

Cool air hit her skin as he dragged them down and over her cheeks. He was now looking at her ass, her too-big ass. Damn it. The man really liked to be understood. "Yes, Sir."

Eric dragged them down to the knees. She could feel them there, almost binding her. One of his hands found the small of her back and held her there.

"Have you spanked a woman before?" Master Alex asked in an academic voice.

There was nothing intellectual and academic about this. This was visceral and real and more intimate than she'd expected.

She was laid out over his knee and waiting. She could barely breathe as she felt the warmth of his big palm cover her cheeks. He stroked her as he answered Master Alex. "Yes. I had a girlfriend who was into the lifestyle. I acquainted myself with BDSM. She was more of a masochist than I liked. I prefer the D/s end of the spectrum. I've been to several clubs but never had any formal training."

He'd been to BDSM clubs? Eric Vail had spanked women before

her. She always wondered how he wasn't married with two point five kids to a woman who made apple pie and sewed all her children's clothing herself. Now she knew. He was busy being a big old perv.

"Then proceed," Master Alex said.

They were all watching. Anxiety knotted her gut and then she couldn't get a breath in because Eric's hand slammed down on her butt. The sound hit her first, a crack that split the air around her, and then fire licked her flesh. He brought his hand down again, four more times in rapid succession. Holy hell that hurt.

He kept his hand on her cheeks, holding the heat there. "How are you doing, Deena? Are you green, yellow, or red?"

In the homework she'd had to do before today's session, she'd learned about the stoplight approach to Dom/sub communication. Red meant she couldn't handle any more, needed the play or discipline to stop immediately. Yellow meant she needed to slow down and green was all is A-okay.

"Deena, I require an answer."

She didn't want him to know she was close to crying. She took a steadying breath. "I'm a yellowy green."

His hand stilled on her, cupping her right cheek even as he steadied her over his lap. "Can I continue? Or do you need a break?"

She could likely get out of this. It was too intimate. She hadn't expected the pain to be so...painful, or the fact that it was Eric giving it to her to be so meaningful. She could feel tears squeezing from her eyelids. How long had it been since she'd allowed herself to cry? She had to be strong. Since the moment Eddie had walked out, she'd told herself she wouldn't shed a tear over what had happened, and she hadn't.

"Please continue. I'm fine." She'd held back for so long she wasn't sure she could let go now.

His hand came down again, and she held on to his leg. The pain flared, flashing through her and making her shake.

"That's right, sweetheart." His voice was calm and flowed over her, reminding her that he was here with her. This wasn't something she was alone in. This was the intimacy of D/s. "Hold on to me. You're doing beautifully. Do you have any idea how gorgeous your ass is? It's beautiful and round and now it's a lovely shade of pink."

He spanked her again and again and finally she felt the tears begin to flow.

She was crying and holding on to the very man who was making her weep. But it wasn't a bad thing. He was giving her something she needed. The tears wouldn't come without this fire and they felt good. The pain she felt somehow opened her up. She lost count, though she suspected Eric hadn't. He wasn't counting out loud, but he was measured and controlled.

With a singular exception. While he might have total control over the rest of his body, she could feel his cock. It had gone hard, and the man had a supersized dick. He had an erection. Her body responded to the feel of that cock against her belly. For the first time in forever, she felt herself get soft and wet even as her ass seemed to be on fire.

One harsh *thwack* ended her punishment and she found herself being lifted up like she weighed absolutely nothing. He set her on her feet and she was happy she hadn't been able to afford to buy new shoes. Subs were given the option of bare feet or stilettos. She was fairly certain if she'd sprung for the heels, she wouldn't have been able to stand. As it was she wobbled a bit.

Eric was right there. He towered over her, his hands coming out to steady her. When she looked up, she was caught by the heat in his eyes, the rigid line of his jaw. Maybe he wasn't as controlled as she'd thought. Maybe this had meant something to him, too. After a moment, he released her and held out a hand. "I'll take those now."

It took her a moment to realize he was talking about her undies. Hell, she'd been so caught up in staring at the man and trying to process what had just happened that she hadn't pulled down her skirt. She tugged it down before stepping out of her undies. Though it seemed such an odd thing to do, she handed them over. He took them and stuffed them in his pocket.

"Do you need a moment, Deena?" Master Liam asked in that lyrical, oh so sexy accent of his.

"He's asking if you need aftercare," Eric explained. He didn't have an Irish accent, but the deep tones of his voice seemed to do something to her insides, making them soft and mushy and willing to do anything the man wanted her to do.

Which was bad. She wasn't sure she could handle aftercare from this man. "I'm good. Let's continue."

He nodded and before she could move back to the rest of the class, he swept her up into his arms. She was cradled against that big chest of his, looking at the scarred side of his face. The long line that cut the right side of his face from above his brow down through his cheek did nothing but enhance how gorgeous and manly he was.

He sat down in one of the empty chairs, settling her on his lap. His arms forced her to curl into him. His big body was so warm, the skin covering his muscles so damn smooth and silky. "You did beautifully, sweetheart."

She let herself relax against him. This was definitely not so bad. When she'd thought about finding a Dom, she was looking for someone who would fulfill her needs to explore her sexuality. Maybe that man could be Eric. If she was careful and didn't get overly involved.

He leaned in and whispered into her ear. "Next time, we'll go somewhere private and I won't let you up until you've had a proper cry. I think you need that, sweetheart. I hated stopping before you got what you needed."

She went stiff in his arms. Yes, this was why she'd stayed away from him. He saw too much, would want far more of her than she would be willing to give.

He was the deep end of the pool and she wasn't ready to jump in.

Master Alex began talking, but all she could think about was the man whose arms surrounded her.

CHAPTER THREE

Eric looked over the boxes that were being sent to McKay-Taggart. Sure they were sandwiches, but they were for Chef's older brother and not so silent partner, Ian Taggart, and his crew. Well, the ones who were at the office. Eric had been overseeing the weekly catered lunches for months, and he knew the names and typical orders by heart. Simon Weston and Jesse Murdoch were apparently on assignment in LA. The only regular orders he hadn't made were Simon's smoked salmon on rye and Jesse's turkey and Swiss. It looked like everyone else was home for the week.

When they catered anywhere but McKay-Taggart, he allowed the line chefs to prep the meals, but that team was special to Sean so he made sure to do it himself.

"Did you pack up the salads?" Javier strode in. He'd made the potato salad himself. It was a special recipe with a nice zing of red pepper. It had been waiting for Eric in the fridge when he'd gotten in this morning. Though Javi was a hot mess when it came to his relationships, the line chef was more than ready to take over for Eric when he left in a few months.

His own place. His own space. He couldn't wait, and after last night, he had some hopes that he wouldn't be going alone.

"I've got them and the soup ready to go." He'd made a chicken tortilla soup and packed individual condiments to go with it. Details were important in his line of work.

They were important in every aspect of his life. Paying attention to details was critical when it came to being in a relationship. Even more important when that relationship included D/s.

Deena had responded beautifully to him the night before. She'd been obviously surprised at first, but then she'd taken that spanking with grace and need. She wasn't playing around as he'd worried. She needed the safety of a D/s relationship and she needed the discipline. She'd been on the edge of a breakthrough and he'd hated to stop. If they'd been alone, he would have spanked her longer. She hadn't fought him at all, hadn't squirmed and begged him to stop. At the end her hand had been holding onto his leg, stroking him and squeezing in a way that encouraged him. She'd needed it, been desperate for it.

He wanted so badly to be the one to give her what she needed.

"So how did it go after the class last night?" Javi asked, his eyebrows waggling salaciously.

Oh, he was shutting that shit down now. "I didn't see her after the class broke off, and I swear I will put you on your ass if you make her feel the slightest bit uncomfortable."

Javi's hands came up. "I promise. I swear on my honor…well, on something else that's way more important. I'm not going to treat her any differently now that I've seen her butt. Same with Tiff. I'm going to pretend like I haven't seen either of their boobs. But seriously, they have great boobs."

"Remember that there's a difference between work boobs and club boobs." It was perfectly fine to look at boobs in the club. It would be a bit rude not to, but there was a time and place.

And Javi wasn't Deena's Dom. Or Tiffany's for that matter. "Did you talk to Mia afterward?"

"She's a nice girl." Javi leaned against the prep table. "I don't know much about her yet."

"I didn't think you needed to know much."

Javi shrugged, giving in on the point. "I don't in order to go to bed with her. This is a little different."

Wow. He sounded serious for once. This was the man who was known for hooking up with three different women in one night at the same club. That had started the single greatest catfight Eric had ever seen, complete with hair pulling and scratching. "Are you actually taking this seriously?"

"I'm not looking for a permanent sub, but I do want to be a good Dom."

"I guess I thought you were doing this for sex."

Javi's lips quirked up. "I'm definitely doing this for sex and that's why I can say with complete confidence, it ain't happening between me and Mia. I know when a chick is into me and she's not. She had all these questions about the lifestyle, and I swear the girl was disappointed when she found out I work at Top and not McKay-Taggart. I think she likes her men on the dangerous side. But I am interested in changing up my sex life. If I keep on the way I am, someone's going to shoot me. Besides, I've got more than enough chaos in my life. I need less and this is a way to organize my social life, so to speak. If I go in with a contract, then a woman is going to know what I can and can't give her. Everything's up front and honest. I think I need some of that in my life."

Javi's home life was completely chaotic. It made sense that he would want the comfort of Sanctum and its contracts.

It wasn't that different from the reasons Eric wanted them or Deena needed them. Like all humans they were damaged and trying to adapt.

He meant to help Deena find that place she needed to find.

"So don't worry that I'm going to make things uncomfortable," Javi finished. "I have to admit I am glad I got Mia and not Tiff. That would be hard, man. Are you sure you can handle working with your sub?"

If he had his way he would do more than work with her. He would spend all his time with her. "We'll be fine."

Javi shook his head. "Really? I'm not a fool, man. I know you've had a thing for this girl since the minute she walked in the door. You think you can make it through training without getting inside that?"

"First of all she's a woman, not a that, and I do not intend to avoid getting into bed with her." He moved the last sack to the table. "Though she did manage to avoid me last night. After tonight's contract session, she's not going to be able to hide anymore."

He had plans. After he'd realized she'd left with Tiffany the previous night, he'd known it was time to set some ground rules.

He had six weeks to convince her. They'd made a great start the night before. It might not be as hard as he'd thought it would be.

The door swung open and the object of his affection walked in. She was in jeans and a T-shirt that hugged her breasts. There was zero chance of him forgetting how pretty she'd been at the club, despite what he'd warned Javi about. The minute he saw her, a picture of her gorgeous ass floated across his mind. And stuck there.

"Hi, sweetheart."

Deena frowned. "Please don't call me that. It's not professional."

Javi backed toward the door to the dining room. "I'm going to go do something else now. Good luck with all that."

Deena looked over the bags. "Is this everything?"

She wasn't looking at him. She hadn't even taken off her sunglasses.

"Deena? Should we talk?" It looked like he'd spoken too soon.

"No reason to talk if you've done your job. I'll do mine and get out of your hair." It appeared the sexy kitten from the night before was gone and in her place was a Deena he'd never seen before.

"Is there a reason you're being so rude?"

Her head finally came up, her mouth a little O. "I wasn't being rude. I'm in a hurry."

"You've got thirty minutes and McKay-Taggart is only fifteen minutes away. And I've called you sweetheart before."

"Only yesterday."

"Fair enough. What's really going on? Is this about last night?"

She flushed, her face turning the sweetest shade of pink. "I don't think we should talk about that at work. Other people could hear. It's why I was shocked to see you and Javier last night. I don't think it's a good idea to mix work and play. Things can get confusing."

"The club is owned by the man you're about to deliver food to." He felt the need to point out a few facts she was overlooking. "Chef is a member of that club. For that matter, Macon and Ally go there, and you're in a class with Tiffany. So I must assume it's only the lesser male employees you object to."

"I don't object," she argued. "I simply think it's going to be weird."

"Do you find me so distasteful?" He was confused. She watched him and not with wary eyes. She doodled his name when she thought no one was looking. What was the problem? He knew she'd been burned, but the training class seemed like the perfect way to bring them together. Unless he'd misread her. "Is it my face?"

He didn't think about it much. He'd gotten torn all to hell during a firefight in South America. His team had been extracting a high-value target when they met with resistance. They'd saved the target but he'd thought for a while he would lose half his face. His whole team had called him Frankenstein for a good six months. Now the scar was simply part of him, but it put some people off.

He thought she'd seen past that. He ached at the idea of Deena thinking he was a freak.

She softened immediately, taking her sunglasses off. She stepped in, her hand drifting up to almost touch his face before she seemed to realize what she was doing. "Don't be ridiculous. The scar is nothing. You're gorgeous and you know it. I'm talking about the fact that we have to work together."

"So we shouldn't play together?" He eased a bit because he believed her about the scar. She wasn't repulsed by him. Anything else was workable. "We've been going out together for months. We go to dance clubs. We've gone to movies. We've hung out."

She shook her head, dark hair moving across her shoulders. "I didn't know that was dating. That doesn't count."

He couldn't help but smile. He moved into her space, happy when she held her ground. "We were hanging out in a group. We're all friends. We work odd hours so it's only natural we would all play together. And when I take you on a date, there won't be any question about what we're doing. I promise."

Now she took a healthy step back, her hand coming up as if to block him. "See. That's what I'm talking about. We can't date. People who work together shouldn't date."

He followed her, paying no attention to that hand. He let her raised palm hit his chest. "Like Chef and his wife? Like Macon and Ally? I won't even go into the very inappropriate relationships at McKay-Taggart."

"They're different."

He put his hand over hers, holding it to him. "How?"

"They're not me."

46

It was time to reassure her. He told himself he wasn't lying. "This isn't dating, Deena. This is a training class that lasts six weeks. We were paired up because the people who run the place thought we would be good training partners. I think we'll be good together, too. I think we proved it last night, but this is only about the six-week training period. This isn't about dating or getting married. It's not that serious."

It wasn't for her. It kind of was for him, but he was a gambling man. If he sat her down and explained to her that he intended to be her only Dom, to be the last man she ever slept with, she would definitely run. Slow and easy was the way to catch this girl. Ease her into a relationship. Get her into bed and show her how well and thoroughly he could please her and then one day she would wake up with a ring on her finger wondering what the hell had gone wrong.

Yeah, that was a good plan.

"It felt serious last night."

He let go of her hand. "So that was why you scampered away after class."

Her chin came up. "I did not scamper anywhere. I left with Tiffany."

"New rule number two is I pick you up and take you home after class."

"I can get a ride with Tiffany," she argued.

"Tiffany is not your Dom for the next six weeks. I am and I will take care of you getting to and from class. Unless you can give me a real reason why you need to ride with Tiffany. Does she have narcolepsy and needs you to wake her up when she falls asleep at the wheel?"

Her lips turned up. "No. Of course not."

"Does she forget the way?"

"You know it's nothing like that." She stared at him as though he should easily know the answer.

The truth was he did know the answer. He simply wasn't sure she was ready to admit what the real problem was. "Then tell me why you don't want me to drive you."

"Because I think you might get handsy at the end of the day."

"Well, maybe I'm afraid you're the one who'll get handsy." He was a little insulted, but he kept his cool. Her fear wasn't about him assaulting her. It was about something else altogether. "I wasn't the one who begged for a spanking last night."

She flushed again. "That is so untrue. I did not beg for a spanking."

"All I'm saying is I can handle myself around you, sweetheart." He moved in close again, backing her up until she was against the metal door of the freezer. She looked like she could handle a cooling off period. He moved in close until his chest almost brushed the curves of her breasts, until his mouth was over hers. "I can spank you and not fuck you. I can top you without ever touching you in a sexual fashion if that's what you're afraid of. If you don't want me to, I'll never kiss you."

"You don't want to kiss me?" The question came out in a husky tone.

"Oh, I want to, but I have control over myself and I want you to think about that. We're together for the next six weeks. We'll sign a contract tonight. We can spend those weeks blandly learning the ins and outs of the club or we can spend them figuring out if we work as sexual partners. I'm lonely, Deena. It's been a long time since I had a lover. I would very much like to spend this time getting to know you in every way I possibly can, but I won't take you if you don't want me back. I can be your Dom and not your lover. I can control my impulses. Hell, I'm always in control, and you should think about that. You should consider the fact that I would use every ounce of that control to bring you pleasure, to take you as high as I can." It was time to pull back. He pushed off the door, having never once touched her. "But it's your choice. In the end, it's always the sub who chooses."

"Why? Why would you want me?" All her arrogance was gone.

"Because we're friends and I like you and you're gorgeous. I've wanted to sleep with you from the moment I saw you. That might not be what you want to hear, but it's the truth. I think we could be good for each other. Neither one of us has had a lover in a long time. Am I right?"

"You're right," she replied. "I haven't even dated anyone since my divorce."

"Then why not try? If it doesn't work, we'll go back to being friends."

Her head shook. "That never happens."

"I don't know what kind of douchebags you've been dating, but I'm still friends with almost every woman I've ever dated. It doesn't have to end in either happily ever after or hate. Especially if we're both honest. The contract is for six weeks. I can promise you right now that I'm still going to like you after six weeks. You be honest with me. Were you planning on experimenting with your training Dom if you'd had chemistry with him? Before you knew I was the Dom. Would you have given that Dom a chance?"

She nodded silently.

"Well, then I suppose we'll have a very abstinent training period and then we'll go our separate ways when it comes to the club. I guess Big Tag and the shrink aren't as smart as they think they are." He wasn't about to give up. This was only the beginning of a very long battle, but it was time to retreat. "We'll talk about the contract later tonight and set up all the rules. I'll still have to touch you during the scenes, but I'll make it as impersonal as possible."

"We don't know that we have chemistry," she said quietly, making no move to grab the bags.

He shrugged. "I guess we won't know."

He turned to begin helping her. He would take the bags out to her car and then let Grace know she was on her way. Someone would meet her in the parking garage to help her bring everything up. He would spend the afternoon planning menus with Chef and heading to the farmer's market to find fresh vegetables for dinner.

A hand on his arm gently pulled and he turned.

Deena was standing right there, her face turned up to him, her eyes wide. "Shouldn't we know?"

She went on her toes and pressed her mouth to his. He went still, unwilling to frighten her away. Soft lips moved over his as her hands found his waist. She was tentative, but he could sense the fire in her. Those hands told the real tale. They moved restlessly, as though she had them on a leash. He wanted that leash taken off.

When she ended the kiss and stared up at him, he decided to go for broke. She wanted to see if they had chemistry? He could show her how volatile they could be.

"My turn," he whispered before he took control. His hands slid up her neck, fingers sinking into the soft, silky strands of her hair.

He kissed her, moving his lips over hers, commanding her. The minute he took control those hands of hers started to move, sliding up the muscles of his back, her body pressing in. He felt her relax as though happy to not be the one in charge. Deena could take control of a room of diners and work that floor with an iron will, but she was shy about this. She needed him to take charge of the physical part.

He could do that. It wouldn't be sexy if she weren't so together in the rest of her life. He kissed her again and again, his tongue finally moving over her full bottom lip. She groaned and her mouth opened, welcoming him inside.

The kiss turned wild, their tongues playing against each other as their bodies came together. He could feel her rubbing against him. He would bet her body was soft, her pussy already getting slick and ready for him.

He was so ready for her.

And if he took her right here on the prep table, she would likely run away forever. She wasn't ready. Not even close.

He broke off the kiss, brushing his lips lightly against hers one last time. He'd promised her control. It was damn iron will that got him to take his hands off her. She was so sweet looking with her hair mussed and her lips puffy from kissing. This was how he wanted to see her all the time. Sweet and willing and ultimately satisfied.

Satisfaction would have to wait.

"We have plenty of chemistry, sweetheart." He kissed the top of her head and stepped back. "It's all going to be fine. I'll take care of everything."

It seemed to take her a moment to come out of her daze. She stared and then shoved her sunglasses back on. "I have to go."

She was out of breath and obviously flustered. That was a good sign. "Let me help you."

She shook her head. "I can get it."

"Deena, I'm going to help you," he ordered, deepening his voice. He was happy when she complied.

* * * *

"Thank god. I'm starving!" Phoebe Murdoch located her lunch with a smile. The rest of the group was milling around, grabbing their orders and getting settled.

A redhead Deena didn't know very well sat down in her seat, her face a complete blank. She had a notebook in front of her and her phone, but she seemed to simply be waiting. Deena looked down at the boxes that were left. Big Tag, Erin, and Master Alex.

Alex McKay. She had to get used to that. One night in Sanctum and she'd had to stop herself from referring to Alex and Liam as Masters.

And Eric. Master Eric. Her Master for the time being. She could still feel his lips, his big body cradling hers. She wasn't sure what she'd been thinking when she'd kissed him. It had been impulsive, but something about the way he'd said the word "chemistry" had made her a little crazy. He said it like he'd known they had chemistry. Like he was an expert. No one knew. Not until they'd tried it.

So she'd kissed him. Yep, they had chemistry like she couldn't believe.

She also likely couldn't handle it. She wanted some pleasure, some experimentation. Eric Vail was the kind of man a girl married, not the kind who fucked her senseless and was happy to let her go at the end of the night.

He was the kind of man she could fall in love with, and she wasn't doing that again. No way. No how. She had to finish the job here and talk to the big guy because this situation wasn't going to work for her. Of course the thought of talking to Master Ian scared the crap out of her.

She picked up the box and walked over to the redhead. Erin. She knew the name. She'd seen Erin a couple of times before at Top, but she'd never had a conversation with her. Deena had seen her with Chef's brother, Theo. Theo Taggart had died a few months back while on a mission. It was hard to believe that happy, laughing man was gone.

"Hey, this one is for you." She set the box down in front of Erin.

Cold eyes glanced up at her. The woman was quite pretty, but there was a chill to her that made Deena want to take a step back. "I didn't order anything and I don't want it. Thank you."

She wasn't sure what to say to that. The name was right there. Someone had ordered it for her. "You have to eat, right?"

A single brow cocked. "No. No, I don't. I don't have to do anything."

Case Taggart moved over to the table. "Yes, you damn well do, Erin. I ordered it and you're going to eat it. You have been eating nothing and I'm done with it. If you want to stay in this meeting, you'll eat everything I ordered for you. Or you can go and have a session with Kai. It's your choice."

Erin's palms flattened against the desk and the whole room seemed to go quiet. "Fine. I'll eat."

She opened the box and took out the sandwich Eric had prepped for her.

Case sighed as though happy the battle hadn't been longer. "It's your favorite. Pulled pork."

Erin shoved it away and stood up quickly, her face going a nice shade of pale. "Eat it your fucking self, Case."

Erin practically ran out the door and down the hall.

Case's eyes closed. "Shit. What do I do now?"

"I could get her something else," Deena offered. It was obvious the woman wasn't into the pork, though Deena happened to know it was delicious.

Grace put a hand on Deena's shoulder. "Don't worry about it. There's nothing wrong with the food. It's simply something we've been worried about. We'll take care of Erin. Why don't you take Ian his lunch? He's not joining the rest of the crew today. He's working on a special project in his office. And don't let him growl at you. He's a pussy cat."

She got the feeling she was being gently but efficiently eased out of the room so the team could start whatever discussion was about to begin. She grabbed Master Ian's box…Ian Taggart's box and stepped out into the hall. She knew where the big guy's office was since she was the one who brought in lunch once a week. He wasn't so scary. He was just a massive, gorgeous man who happened to know how to kill a person forty different ways and was famous for his sarcastic outlook on life. And for being a hard-ass Master with every sub in the world but his wife.

It would be fine. She would explain the problem and he would be reasonable. After all, the D/s world was built on communication. Even the night before, Master Alex and Master Liam had lectured about the importance of Dom and sub communication. How could the Dom know what the sub wanted if she never told him? How could the sub understand the Dom's needs if they weren't explained?

She needed a new Dom because she was far too invested in the current one for her peace of mind. How could Master Ian know that if she never told him?

Also, she had slipped a slice of lemon cheesecake in with his lunch. Everyone knew the big guy liked Macon's desserts.

It was going to be all right. She would explain the situation to Master Ian and then she and Eric could go back to being normal, absolutely no chemistry between them coworkers.

She knocked on his door.

"Come in," came the deep-voiced command.

That man used his Dom voice twenty-four seven from what she could tell. There wasn't a lot of difference between Big Tag, the boss, and Master Ian, the Dom.

She opened the door and the man himself was sitting behind his massive desk, his eyes on the computer in front of him. Behind him were floor to ceiling windows with a spectacular view of Dallas.

Taggart didn't look up from his computer. "Did Erin eat her lunch?"

Wow. It looked like the whole crew was very into that poor woman eating something. "Uh, no."

His eyes came up, holding her.

"No, Sir. She did not."

Taggart sat back. He was wearing a dark T-shirt, his hair a tad longer than a military cut, but it was easy to see the soldier in the way he held himself. "Did she give you a reason?"

"Not really. She yelled at your brother, opened the box, and then I don't think she liked what she saw. She kind of ran out of the room. But she did manage to yell at your brother again. I told Grace that I could get Erin something else. I can go back to Top and be back here in about thirty minutes."

Taggart's eyes closed and he seemed to be thinking for a moment. "No. She doesn't want anything. Don't worry about it. Let's say it was a bit of an experiment and I have the intel I need." His eyes came open, staring at the box. "What did Sean send? Did my wife change my order? Because she sometimes does that. She's got it in her head that I should eat salads. Do I look like a bunny rabbit to you?"

Nope. He looked like a big old lion who could tear through a gazelle in a heartbeat, and she unfortunately knew what was in his lunch. "No, Sir. Like I said, I can just run back to Top."

"Damn it." Taggart slapped his desk. "That woman is going to drive me insane." He picked up his phone. "Grace? I want you to clear Charlie's schedule for this afternoon because she's getting the spanking of a lifetime." There was a pause. "Some kind of damn salad. And make sure daycare knows we'll be late." He slammed the phone down. "At least tell me it's got some meat on it and not fish."

She rushed forward, happy to give the man some good news. "Jerk chicken."

Taggart threw his head back and laughed. "Yeah, she's getting another fifty for that. Thank you."

She set the box on his desk. "I was hoping to speak with you, Sir."

"Then all of your hopes have come true since we are indeed speaking." Taggart went back to looking at his computer.

She couldn't see the computer screen but he had a bunch of maps on his desk. It looked like the Caribbean and several islands. They were marked up in a new grid pattern, as though he was searching for something.

She hoped he'd found it because she'd already disappointed him once with the salad. "I'm a new trainee at Sanctum."

"Congratulations. I'm sure you'll be very happy there getting your ass smacked by various and sundry Doms. Have fun."

He was a frustrating man.

"I needed to talk to you about that."

"You should talk to your Dom. I assume you have a training Dom. Alex is usually very thorough about not letting the subs roam free range for the first six weeks."

"My training Dom is the problem."

Now she had his attention. Those deep blue eyes were focused on her, his jaw a harsh line. "He's done something he shouldn't? That was quick. It usually takes the assholes a few days to show their true colors. You were paired with Eric Vail. I didn't see that coming. I would have told you he would make an excellent Dom. Sean is going to be upset. I'll need to know exactly what he's done."

She shook her head and took the seat in front of him. She didn't want to get Eric in trouble with Chef. "No. It's nothing bad. Eric is a great guy. I mean he did spank me, but I agreed to it."

Ian's brow cocked. "You were first day spanking girl?"

Damn, she already had a nickname. "I'm afraid so. Master Alex pretty much demanded it."

"If you pissed off Alex on the first day, you likely deserved whatever Master Eric gave you," Taggart stated flatly. "So what is the problem? Did you disapprove of his spanking method? Are you a connoisseur? What exactly do we call those? Spankpert? Do you have a checklist of how you need to be disciplined when you get out of line? Perhaps Master Eric needs one of those. Put some glitter on it so he can't miss the salient points."

Wow, those words were icy cold coming out of his mouth. When that man got pissy he could practically frost over a room. "I didn't have a problem with the spanking. It was fine. I had been rude and I agreed to all the parameters of discipline at Sanctum. The problem is Eric himself. I don't think we can work together."

Taggart went still as he watched her. "Do you have a degree in psychology? Because the man who paired you up with Master Eric does. Several of them, in fact. Are you telling me Master Kai has made a mistake and you know of a better partner for you? Because I believe you plainly stated that you had no preference and would be eager to work with any of the Doms."

That was because she'd never dreamed Eric would be there. "Master Kai is brilliant, I'm sure, but I would be more comfortable with someone else."

Taggart sighed. "Good. I'm glad you felt like you could express that feeling, and I think you should look forward to lots of spankings in your future. You can go now."

She stood up. That had been easier than she thought. "Okay. So, I'll meet the new training Dom tonight?"

Taggart was back to looking at his maps while he unpacked his lunch. He grimaced at the salad, but picked up the fork anyway. "Not at all. You can accept the Dom who was given to you or you can leave the program. Welcome to Sanctum and all that."

What had the man misunderstood? "But I can't be with him. I can't. I have to work with him so I can't have a relationship like that with him. He's kind of my superior. I think that would be inappropriate."

"It sounds perfectly appropriate to me. He bosses you around at work. Now he bosses you around in the club. You should be used to it."

She could feel the beginnings of tears because he wasn't listening to her. "I don't think it's going to work."

"Then the door is right there. Feel free to walk out it."

She stood. This was useless. There was no moving him. It looked like she was going to have to leave the program. She turned to walk out.

"I hate crying females. I guess I hate crying anyones. Except for Adam. It's fun when Adam cries. And the twins. I can't ever hate them. Stop and tell me why you don't want Eric as your Dom. You've got exactly one minute to tell me the truth and if you don't, I'll let you walk out and you won't be welcome back. Don't bullshit me about him being your boss."

Her stomach was in knots. "I don't want to care about him."

"All right. I believe that. Is it only him or any male you don't want to care about?"

A very good question. "Any, I suppose. I was married and I don't want to do that again. I don't want to do any of that again."

"Then maybe a club where people do kinky sex things is not for you," Taggart said. "Might I suggest a nunnery? I think there are a few of those left."

She nearly groaned her frustration. "I want to have sex. Sex isn't the problem. Well, it was one of the problems with my marriage, and that's why I want to explore it. I don't want to have a relationship."

He nodded as though he finally understood. "All right. I'm sure someone can find the number of a male escort service for you."

"That's not what I want at all." How did anyone deal with this obnoxious man?

"Let me see if I can figure this out, Deena. You want sex without emotion. I don't know that you'll find what you're looking for with Sanctum's brand of D/s. Certainly not since all the asshole Doms went and found the feels and shit. Li was your best shot and he's all about his wife now. Communication is important and that means getting to know a person. Contrary to popular belief, you won't find hundreds of unattached Doms willing to service your sexual needs. There are maybe ten Doms without subs. What happens when you run through them?"

She stared right back at him now because she wasn't going to take that. Not from anyone. "I thought you were different. I thought I wouldn't get slut shamed at a place like Sanctum."

A long sigh came from Taggart and he sat back. "I wasn't shaming you. I don't care how much uninvolved sex you have. It likely won't touch what I did when I thought my wife was dead. I was only pointing out a few problems with your plan. My point is that you will get to know all of these men. You'll get friendly with them and you will develop feelings for them because you're human and that's what we do even when we don't want to. If you weren't capable of caring, Kai would have disapproved your application. Me? Now I think every club needs a cold-ass bitch, but every time I bring one in, my wife kicks her ass. If you're looking for a quick, anonymous hookup, you should go to a bar because the men I bring into Sanctum will try to take care of you, and that seems like something you don't want."

"You're twisting my words." She didn't like the way it sounded when Taggart said it. She thought of it as fun and carefree, but he was right that she was afraid of the emotional aspect of sex. It was all so confusing.

"Am I? Or do you simply not know what you want? Look, I've read your file. You went through a shitty divorce and you've decided no one is ever going to do you wrong again. You won't accept a relationship where you could get hurt. But I'm asking you if you intend to go through the rest of your life without ever trying. And what's next? Because I've found that when you cut yourself off from one form of relationship, you get harder on the others. So when a friend fails you next, will you cut all of them off? Because if those are your intentions, skip the Sanctum membership and start collecting cats."

He was starting to make her mad. Though she'd signed on as a sub, she wasn't willing to simply keep her mouth shut. "You don't have to be so harsh. If you don't want me in your club, I don't have to be there."

"I've got room in my life for one stubborn bitch right now and it's not you. I selected you because Sean thought Sanctum would be good for you. I thought it would be good for you. Kai thinks you need it to find yourself. But it doesn't sound like you want to find yourself. It sounds like you're trying to hide from the world. Do it on someone else's time. I just lost my brother. He doesn't get the chance to find himself. I'm spending my days marking grid patterns so I can pay a group to search the fucking ocean for his body. You don't want to allow a damn decent man to train with you, fine." He stood and sighed. "Damn it. Now you're really crying."

"I tend to do that when people are mean to me." She wished she could be cool and calm like other people, but her natural reaction was to tear up. It was something her ex-husband had complained about. *Why do you have to be so emotional, Deena? Can't you ever be logical?*

It was why she never let herself cry anymore. Last night had done a number on her. Being spanked by Eric seemed to have opened something up inside her that would better be left locked away.

Taggart moved across the room toward her, that bleak visage lightening marginally. He stood in front of her, big hands on her shoulders. "I'm sorry, Deena. I'm under a lot of pressure and you're not a fair target. Give it a chance with Eric. No one else in the group was right for you. He'll be patient and understanding."

"And what if I give in?"

"I'm going to say something to you that I say to everyone who has this problem. Don't sleep with him. It's very simple. Go into this experience with an open mind and locked knees. You should be fine.

58

Though you should know a good Dom can get through those locked knees. And please forgive me for being unkind. I am many things, but I hope I'm not that. Losing my brother has been hard on my sense of humor."

She sniffled and wiped her tears. She'd never had a brother. She was an only child and now it seemed she was intent on isolating herself further. The idea that she was being hard on the people around her might not be so wrong. Walls could protect but they could also keep out good things. "I'm sorry I'm being so inflexible. And I put a slice of lemon cheesecake in your box, but I think you should eat the salad because I've met your wife and she scares me more than you do."

Taggart laughed and she was happy she could put a smile on the man's face. He walked back to his desk and sat down again. "I will eat my jerk chicken salad and then share my cheesecake with a couple of babes. I mean that literally. My twins are madly in love with solid food. I can't tell you what that does to a diaper."

She didn't want to know. She couldn't handle a pet much less a kid.

Maybe she could handle Eric. It would all come down to communication. "Thanks, Sir."

"And Deena," Taggart called out as she began to leave. "Remember when I told you I tell everyone not to sleep with their partners? No one ever listens."

She intended to be the first.

CHAPTER FOUR

Eric stopped what he was doing and stared at Javier. "You can't be serious. She wouldn't do that."

Javier was busy chopping peppers, his hands moving at lightning speed. "I'm telling you what I heard. Big Tag told his wife, who mentioned it to Grace, who called Chef, and I overheard that conversation."

His best friend did have some issues. "You eavesdropped on our boss?"

Javier never missed a beat. "I eavesdrop on everyone. It's a hobby. How do you expect to run your own place if you don't listen in on your employees? You have to stay on top of that shit. Like I happen to know that two of the busboys are having an affair, and it's not who you would think."

He hadn't thought any of them would have an affair. "With each other?" That wasn't the point and he wasn't going to get into the soap opera that played out in every restaurant he'd ever worked in. He was concerned with his own little drama. "She tried to dump me as her training Dom?"

It made him feel like he'd gotten kicked in the stomach. He knew she'd been in a bit of shock after the kiss they'd shared. When he'd helped her pack up her car, she'd been quiet and unable to meet his eyes, but he'd expected her to bounce back the way she always did. He'd explained that he would pick her up after he got off work and she'd nodded and taken off. She wasn't working the dinner shift so he would have to wait until later to see her.

To ask her how she could possibly have tried to dump him after that kiss.

"She apparently tried to get them to assign her to someone else and Big Tag said no, so the man has your back," Javi said.

Why was he pushing this so hard? The woman didn't want him. He should accept that and move on.

There were other fish in the sea. Lots of them. Hell, he could likely even date someone here if he amped up the charm.

He turned back to his ovens, checking the timer for the hundredth time. "I'll talk to him myself. If she wants another Dom, she can have one."

He'd been looking forward to tonight. They were supposed to sit together and go over the standard contract before writing in their own clauses. They were supposed to start to talk about what they both needed. He'd been looking forward to that. He'd talked to her many times over the past year. He knew a lot about her. He knew her parents had split up when she was young and she hadn't seen her father much after that. She'd been raised by a hard-working single mother who she loved dearly and talked to at least twice a week. She wanted a dog, but her apartment didn't allow pets. He'd studied her, but they'd never talked about sex. It hadn't been appropriate. The conversation tonight would be all about sex.

Would have been.

"You're giving up pretty easily," Macon said.

Eric hadn't heard the big pastry chef come in. He turned and noticed Macon was accompanied by the new guy. Chef had recently brought in a sommelier. Sebastian Lowe was a tall, elegant man who seemed to think a three-piece suit was proper attire for a kitchen. He looked somewhat out of place amongst the crew of Top. Chef tended to hire ex-military men and Sebastian didn't fit the bill, but according to his resume he was one of four master sommeliers in the entire state of Texas. He'd only been working for a few weeks, but he was quiet and efficient, never spending too much time with anyone on the staff with the exception of Macon.

"Do you have my plates ready?" Sebastian asked in his slow, Southern accent.

Sebastian was given a tasting plate of every item on the menu for the night and he paired the wines from there. He insisted on tasting even dishes he'd had before because according to him tiny variations in a recipe made a difference to his perfect palate.

"I set them out on the prep table for you," Eric explained. After Sebastian had nodded and moved to the plates, Eric turned back to Macon. It looked like Javi wasn't the only one who listened in. "What am I supposed to do? I can't force her to be my partner."

"Big Tag already did that for you," Javi pointed out.

Macon leaned over and picked up one of the perfectly sliced green pepper strips, popping it into his mouth and munching before continuing. "Those have an excellent flavor. And Javi's right. The hard work's been done. Now you have to prove yourself."

"And if she walks out?" He wasn't sure that he could be the reason she was forced to walk away. He'd seen how excited she'd been the night before. She wanted to try this. She just didn't want to try it with him.

"She won't," Macon assured him. "Look, don't tell Ally I told you this, but Deena came by after she dropped off lunch at McKay-Taggart. She told Ally that Big Tag is an asshole—stop the presses—but that he made sense and she kind of ended up liking him, so she's going to give it a shot tonight. You have your six weeks with her."

They were a big old group of gossips and thank god for that. Still, after that kiss they'd shared, he'd been absolutely sure she would give them a shot. Instead, she'd gone straight to the big boss and asked for a change. "I don't know. I might be opening myself up for a whole lot of heartache."

"She's not an easy nut to crack," Macon replied. "She's been through a lot."

Javi looked up. "Yeah, what's up with that girl? She's so nice to everyone, but then she seems to push people away when they try to get close."

"You tried to get close?" He could hear the hardness of his own voice. Yes, he got jealous. He was only human and Deena was a beautiful woman. Javi was six foot, well-muscled, and all Latin lover. More than one woman had found herself locked in a closet with Javi before she truly knew what she was doing.

Javi rolled his dark eyes. "Don't get your back up. I asked her some personal stuff one night. About her ex. She got cold really fast."

Javi obviously hadn't done the same snooping Eric had. "She got married straight out of high school and put her asshole husband through law school. He promptly dumped her for a woman he met at his new firm."

Macon stared for a moment. "Stalker."

"I asked a few questions and did a little digging. I was curious."

"Well, you're right, but it's worse than that," Sebastian said, reminding everyone that he was there.

Eric turned toward him. He was finishing up his tasting and writing down some notes on a clipboard. "How would you know? You've been here a month."

"*In vino veritas*," Sebastian said. His sandy blond hair was slicked back, his clothes maintaining a perfection Eric would never know. He could wrinkle a T-shirt in four point five seconds. "When the rep from Hanover wines came in, she helped me taste. She didn't understand the idea of taste and spit."

"You spit out the wine?" Javi asked, horrified.

Sebastian shook his head as though they were all barbarians. "I can try up to a dozen vintages in one tasting. Yes, I spit it out. Otherwise my senses would be dead by the time I got to the later bottles. Deena had fun with it. And she flirted with the rep."

"That's great to know," Eric said. She liked wine reps.

"So she talked to you after the tasting?" Macon seemed to be determined to get past Eric's jealousy.

Thank god he had a sensible friend. He needed to shut that shit down or he would scare her off. "What did she talk about?"

"She's a lightweight. She got flirtier after the fifth taste. She was drinking roughly a quarter of a glass each time. The funny thing was when he asked her out, she seemed horrified and apologized," Sebastian said. "I drove her home. She talked about her ex-husband. They grew up together, dated in high school. She didn't realize how much he was changing until he walked in one day and told her he'd grown out of the marriage. He'd had all these experiences that she'd made possible, but because she spent all her time on him, she'd stayed the same. His new girlfriend decided she didn't want a husband with all that debt. She hired her father, who is one of the biggest bully divorce lawyers in town, and they gave Deena an ultimatum. She could agree to a simple fifty fifty division of their assets or they would tie her up in court for years and she would have to pay the attorney fees. And they managed to freeze their accounts. So Deena had nothing to fight with."

He would love to meet her ex. "She should have been given a good portion of his earnings for the next several years. She gave up her own education to support him."

"The state of Texas doesn't acknowledge what she put into the marriage," Sebastian said, putting his notebook down. "There are no provisions for alimony for a woman like Deena. She can support herself so the court wouldn't have given her alimony. What they might have given her was a break. All the debt for his law school was secured with her name and her job. All their debt was joint. By taking the deal, she had to agree to pay off seventy thousand dollars worth of debt."

"She sold everything she had and it still took her five years and two jobs to do it," Macon said quietly.

"Damn, man, where I come from there's a simple solution to that. It's called life insurance. She should have killed him before he left her and collected," Javi said with a sad shake of his head. "Seriously. I know a guy."

Javier knew a lot of interesting people, but it was a bit late to collect on her ex's policy. "Macon, you knew about this?"

"I knew she was paying off debt," Macon replied, giving Sebastian a long look. "I didn't think that was anyone else's business."

Sebastian frowned. "Well, I was trying to fit in. You told me I should do that. It seems to me that the men in the kitchen like to gossip. Besides, she also talked about Eric. I believe the word she used was hottie. I do not believe she was discussing your cooking."

He knew she was attracted to him. That wasn't enough. Not even close. Attraction wasn't what he was looking for. "That doesn't mean she wants me. I like this woman. I want more than a one-night stand with her."

Sebastian looked thoughtful for a moment. "Having spoken with her that night, I think she wants you as well. She can try to say it's all about sex, but I don't think she's the type. Men make moves on her all the time, but she brushes them off. Many of those men are very attractive by today's standards. She's not interested. She can giggle about men with Tiffany and Ally, but it never goes past that. Sometimes what a person wants and what they need are two different things. It's like a perfectly paired wine. You make an excellent crab bisque, but I've noticed you ignore my pairing."

"I prefer the Sauvignon Blanc. It's what I usually drink with fish." He wasn't a major fan of sommeliers. He liked a couple of wines. He preferred to concentrate on the food.

"Try it. Take a good spoonful of the bisque and then take a drink of this wine." Sebastian uncorked one of the bottles he was holding and poured a small amount of the rich looking gold wine.

He sighed. He did not need a lecture on wine pairings, but when he opened his own place, Sebastian had agreed to help with the wine list. He wouldn't get a better offer so he wasn't about to piss the man off. He knew what his damn crab bisque tasted like, but he took a spoonful anyway. The flavor coated his mouth, creamy and rich, with the buttery meat of the crab. He took the glass from Sebastian and swallowed a mouthful.

It complemented the crab, drawing out the flavor in a way the wine he would have used never could have. He stopped for a moment and savored the taste. Sometimes it was easy to forget why he'd started down this path. Food was a passion for him. It was something he loved, needed in his life. When had he stopped experimenting? He put down the glass and faced Sebastian. "That was perfect."

"We get into comfortable places and forget to try new things," Sebastian said quietly.

"I think what he's trying to say is don't get your panties in a wad and be patient," Javi said with a nod. "Deena will come to you."

"I never mentioned his panties." Sebastian recorked the wine with a sad shake of his head. "Macon, I'll be in the cellar. I need to check on how the new order was stocked. The last time I walked in there someone had put a Pinot Noir in the refrigerated section. Barbarians."

He turned and walked out.

"That is one weird dude," Javi said with a shake of his head. "And he was totally talking about your panties. All that wine stuff was a metaphor."

Macon laughed. "He's a good guy. I knew him for a while in the Army."

Eric nearly dropped his jaw. "Sebastian Lowe was in the Army? Was he in your unit?"

"No. I met him in rehab. He walks pretty good for a dude who lost his legs, doesn't he? He's also a legend in sommelier land. It takes decades for some people to reach master status. He's the youngest in the country. I know he comes off as weird, but give him a break. He's completely transformed himself. And he had offers to work in France, New York, and LA. Do you know why he chose to come to work for an upstart chef in Texas?"

Damn, he needed to give his coworkers the benefit of the doubt. "He wanted to be with his people."

He wanted to be with the ex-soldiers and they'd kind of crowded the man out because he was different. That would change and fast.

"I hear what you're saying and I'll make sure to include him. I'll put the word out." He shook Macon's hand. "I'll also take his advice and try to not get my panties in a wad."

He would take another look at Deena, try to give her what she needed, and stop worrying about his damn ego. She'd been through hell. It hadn't been a short journey. It would take time to teach her she didn't have to stay there.

* * * *

Deena sat across from her Dom. The reality was starting to settle in. After her talk with Master Ian, she'd realized she was taking all of this far too seriously. It was all play. It was experimentation. It didn't matter who her training Dom was. She looked around and watched the other couples. She would bet Tiffany wasn't worried about getting in too deep with the man she'd been paired with. Althea was talking calmly to her new sub, not a hint of panic or terror on her placid face. And the chick Javi had been partnered with better not think it could go anywhere. The man had a broom closet at Top with his name etched on it from his many quickies. No, she was the only one panicking and there was zero reason for it.

Eric was her training Dom, or at least he would be once they signed this contract. It didn't mean anything more than they were compatible on some level. She stared down at it. They'd gone over hard and soft limits. She was interested in just about everything but the truly extreme stuff. She'd happily checked off her interest in role-playing, bondage, fire and electric play. Those last two were a little scary, but she couldn't help but shiver at the thought. Why not try it? The great thing about D/s was she had a safe word. If things got dicey, she said the word "red" and everything stopped.

Of course, having a Dom who she knew one hundred percent would honor her safe word was also good.

She'd thought about it all day. After the talk with Master Ian, she'd gone over to Ally's. Ally had convinced her it would be good to work with a Dom who would have no expectations of her sexually.

Deena hadn't mentioned the fact that he'd kissed her. He'd kissed like she'd never been kissed before. He'd inhaled her like he needed her in order to breathe. She could still feel his tongue sliding against hers, dominating her.

"Deena?" His deep voice broke through her thoughts. "Have I lost you? Or are you seriously thinking about checking the humiliation play box? You should read the section thoroughly before you do that."

She gasped and quickly marked the box no. She didn't judge. If some women got off on being called a dirty whore or getting peed on during sex, cool. Whatever floated someone's boat got a thumbs-up from her, but she was not doing that. "I'll pass."

His lips turned up in the hottest grin. "That's good because I'll be honest, I'm not very interested in exploring that either."

Of course not. He wouldn't ever call a woman a whore. He was safe. That was what Ally had convinced her of. Eric was a safe bet. Unless she initiated contact or stepped way out of line, he would be a simple play partner who could introduce her to this world, and then she could find a dirty Dom who would take only what she was willing to give.

"Do you have any questions for me?" Eric asked as she finished the questionnaire portion of the contract.

All around her the other training couples were sitting and talking. Tiffany was grinning at something and pointing it out to her training Dom. Althea was super cool and mysterious, while her trainee looked so out of place. He was a big, gorgeous male hunk who looked like he should be on the other end of the crop.

They were all trying to find themselves. She had to remember that. Focus on the journey and not the man in front of her. That was the mistake she'd made before. She'd thought the man was the journey when he'd been the roadblock.

She smiled and shook her head and signed her name on the dotted line. "No, I think I'm good."

His grin faded, but he took the contract anyway. "All right. Let's go over the opening documents. We're supposed to talk about our expectations and what we're both hoping to get out of this class."

She'd disappointed him. It was plain on his face, but she wasn't sure how she'd done it. She'd signed the contract, agreed to sub for him through the training class. Did it matter? If he wanted something from her, he was supposed to ask.

They'd spent the first half of the class talking about how she'd gotten here. He'd asked about her childhood, polite questions about where she'd grown up and how she'd ended up in Dallas. She'd been honest, though she'd dodged some of the worst aspects of her life. He knew she'd been married and divorced. She'd explained her husband had left her for another woman. That was all he needed to know. They'd wasted half an hour on her boring life before getting to the contract.

"What do you expect to get out of this class?" He was warm, but she could feel a distance that hadn't been there before.

"Knowledge, I suppose. I want what everyone wants. I want to figure out if I enjoy this lifestyle. I think I will."

"What about it attracts you?"

This was something she'd thought long and hard about. "I started reading some BDSM romance books about a year ago. I did it because Tiffany recommended it, and honestly, I was curious because the author comes into Top all the time."

"Serena. I like her a lot. I haven't read her books, but she's a very nice lady."

Serena Dean-Miles was funny and kind. "I thought I could joke about it. You know, look at me I'm reading porn."

"It spoke to you."

She nodded. "Yes. I've never read romance before. She had something to say about finding ourselves, about paying attention to our own needs in a way that wasn't selfish. I suppose I grew up with a mother who sacrificed everything for me, and don't get me wrong, I appreciate all that she did for me. But I know she was unhappy. I knew it then. I wonder what would have happened if she'd pursued some of her own joy. She was a wonderful woman, but I felt her dissatisfaction. I think I thought that was how the world had to work for a very long time."

"That's why you sacrificed in your marriage."

Touchy subject, but somehow she found herself opening up. No, Eric didn't need to know these things, but sitting in this room where she was supposed to be open and honest, she found herself talking. "I think it was a lot of things. Despite the fact that my dad was a jerk, I remember hearing them fight a lot. He would accuse her of not paying enough attention to him. He said he was leaving her because he'd found a woman who supported him better than she did. A woman who made him feel like a man. I know he was wrong, but sometimes the things we hear as children seem to seep into our psyches."

Eric leaned forward. "It's a two-way street. Support that is. I'm not saying in a relationship everything should be fifty-fifty at all times. Needs change. They ebb and flow and a couple has to be fluid, but one person shouldn't bear the load. Why do you have a partner at all if you're going to do that?"

"That's a good question and why I won't get married again." She'd made that decision long ago.

"So even if the right man came along, you wouldn't try?"

"Probably not. I'm not putting myself in that position again. You wouldn't understand because you've never been married before."

He sat back, his arms crossing over his chest. "Who said I hadn't been married before?"

"You never mentioned an ex-wife."

"You never asked."

Wow. She hadn't. He'd asked her a million questions about her life and she never asked him anything but superficial crap. They'd been friends for months and she knew next to nothing about his past. She'd seen his gorgeous body and face and dismissed him utterly with the exception of enjoying his company on a surface level.

What had Master Ian told her? When a person cuts off one kind of relationship, she inevitably becomes harder on all the others. She'd cut off the possibility of love. Had she done the same with friendship? Was she going to end up cutting them all out because she was so scared of hurting again?

She was living her mother's life.

"I never did, did I?" Shame swept over her. He'd been kind and she'd blown him off. She spent time daydreaming about the man and yet she refused to let herself know him. Even tonight he'd concentrated on her and she'd ignored his needs, expecting that he would simply take care of them himself.

She was being a bad partner.

"It's all right," he said quietly. "You've made it plain you aren't interested in more than a training relationship."

But they'd had more. This was the guy who helped her out when he didn't have to. He gave her a ride and sat next to her in clubs, though she wasn't sure he truly enjoyed them. The man never danced, but insisted on going along with them to make sure everyone got home all right. He looked out for her and she viewed him as nothing more than a gorgeous guy she should stay away from.

"I thought we were friends."

"I did, too."

"I haven't been a very good friend." That bothered her. She was good to her girlfriends. She always had an open couch. Even when she was struggling she could find the money to help out a friend. Eric had proven he was loyal and kind, and she hadn't given anything back to him. It was one thing to not fall in love with the man. It was another to be unkind to him. Had she made him feel small? "Have you ever been married, Eric? I mean, Sir."

"Eric is fine when we're talking. Sir or Master Eric when we're playing or in formal club circumstances, but we are friends. I'm sorry. I didn't mean to make you feel bad about that. And yes, I was married. Like you, I married my high school sweetheart."

She hadn't seen that coming. He was so open. She'd expected he hadn't been hurt before. "What happened?"

"Oh, years away in the Navy happened. We changed and we weren't together when we changed, so I came home to a different woman than the one I married. She married a kid who liked sports and sneaking beers and I came home angry and scared."

"Of war?"

"Of how much I liked it. Not the killing. I liked the camaraderie. I liked being important. I was good at it. I was so good at it I went Special Forces. She thought she'd married a kid who was in the Navy to get his college degree paid for and she found herself married to a SEAL."

She didn't understand how that had caused a rift. "That doesn't sound so bad. You were serving your country."

"Like you said, sweetheart, you haven't lived it. We married young and we both had to move on. I wish she hadn't moved on while I was on active duty, but I understand."

"She cheated on you while you were fighting?" Who the hell did that? Outrage rose in her gut. He'd been risking his life.

"Well, it wasn't like she knew how to get hold of me," he said with a soft laugh, as though the incident was amusing. "My whereabouts were classified and I would go months sometimes without talking to her. She was lonely and she turned to someone else."

"You didn't." Eric Vail wouldn't cheat on his wife.

His eyes narrowed thoughtfully. "Why do you say that?"

"Because you're not that guy."

"No, sweetheart. I'm not that guy. I was faithful to my wife. I'm friendly with her now. She's married again and has a couple of kids."

"How can you still talk to her?" She wouldn't talk to her ex for anything.

"Because we were friends before we were anything else. I've learned life is far too short to hold grudges. It's too short to not forgive yourself."

"You didn't do anything wrong."

"Didn't I? There are two sides to every story. I didn't come home

71

when I said I would. Once I forgave myself for making the mistake, I found it was quite easy to forgive her for doing the same. I left the service after one too many bullets hit me and I found something I really loved."

"Cooking."

"Yeah. It's funny because I wouldn't have found it if May hadn't left me and I hadn't been forced to move back to my folks' place after I got home. My mom was crazy about cooking shows and she challenged me to try it. I indulged her, and a few months later, I was at a cooking school with all these tiny young people. They were infants. Most of them thought I was the janitor the first day. Or maybe security. I thought a lot about my sister while I was there. She was older than me and she loved to bake. She was always making cookies."

He said it with a sad smile that made her wonder. "Is she a chef, too?"

"She died when I was sixteen. Leukemia. I took that cooking challenge from my mother because I knew she missed my sister and wanted a child of hers in the kitchen with her again. Even if it was only for a day. I cook with my mom any time I'm home, and let me tell you I might be the pro, but I'm her sous chef, too. She rules that kitchen with an iron will any chef would be proud of. If I hadn't gone into the Navy, hadn't gotten married and divorced, I wouldn't have been sitting with her that day. I wouldn't have laughed and said it looked easy. I wouldn't have found my passion. Those things that seemed like mistakes led me to something I love. So I forgave myself and moved on."

How hard had it been for him to go from soldier to chef? From married to single and happy? He seemed so happy, she'd imagined he never faced a single moment of pain. That was arrogant of her. He was a man, and every single man born had been through pain. She needed to stop thinking of him in terms of how gorgeous he was and see past that.

The trouble was everything she learned about the man made him that much more dangerous.

He was stronger than she was. She couldn't forgive her ex. She simply couldn't. The wound felt so fresh. Perhaps after she'd started her own career and moved on, she could forget about the pain he'd dealt her. She wasn't sure she would ever take that risk again. But maybe she could be friends with Eric. Real friends.

They were stuck together for six weeks. She glanced back down at the contract. Part of the contract stated plainly that both parties agreed to touching and displays of affection. She hadn't marked that out. She'd agreed to allowing him to touch her if it felt right and good to both parties.

She reached out and put her hand over his. "I'm sorry to hear about your sister."

He flipped his hand over, lacing their fingers together. His big palm swallowed and warmed hers. "I miss her. You would have liked her."

Oh, she already liked one of the Vail siblings way too much. His hand wrapped around hers, their fingers all tangled. She liked that too much as well. It felt…right. "I'm sure I would. I don't have any siblings. I always wondered what it would be like to have a sister."

He started talking about his family and she couldn't help but watch the way his face lit up. He always seemed so serious, but there was a mirth, a mischievousness that she hadn't seen in him before. He told her how he and his sister would fish in the pond behind their house, how she'd had to bait his hook because he couldn't stand touching the worms.

Deena hadn't had that childhood connection. Her mother had moved a lot. She'd gone to five different elementary schools and two junior highs. They'd settled in a suburb for her high school tenure, but she never quite quit expecting to have to up and leave.

She loved her friends, but had she been this honest with them? As Eric talked she realized she hadn't told anyone her story. She talked about innocuous things, about the superficial. She listened. Oh, she was a great listener. She would listen to anyone, with the singular exception of the one man who mattered. She'd withheld that from him the same way she withheld herself from everyone.

She was still the new kid in school, unsure of her place and therefore hiding behind superficiality.

"It must have been nice to grow up in one place. Do your parents still live there?" Now that he was talking, she was curious. This was why she hadn't asked. She'd known she would be interested, that learning about Eric Vail would be a slippery slope. But he seemed so happy that she couldn't draw back.

And she had kind of signed a contract stating she might just maybe have sex with him. If they both wanted to. If it came up. Which it probably wouldn't.

He picked up the pen and signed his name before looking up at her again. He smiled, a look of satisfaction on his face. "Come here. I'll tell you everything you want to know, but I believe I mentioned that there are no chairs for you here."

She was supposed to sit in his lap. She'd signed a contract to obey him and part of that was sitting in his lap. All last night she'd thought about how good it had felt to curl up on his lap and not worry about anything.

He held out a hand and she had to make a decision. The night before it had been easy. She'd been warm from the spanking, her whole body relaxed and oddly sated. Now she realized she had to make the conscious choice to submit to this man, to give over to his will. A scary prospect because she didn't always make good choices.

But this one was already made. She'd made it when she signed the contract.

Deena got up out of her chair and moved to her new Dom. He wouldn't be hers for long, and that could be the thing that saved her. This relationship had an end date, a clear and precise one. Six weeks. They would only be together for a month and a half. There was some safety in that. She might be able to get Eric Vail out of her system in six weeks, and then she would be free to move on with her life without regretting him.

She sank onto his lap, his arms going around her. He was so big that it wasn't hard to get comfortable sitting on his lap. It also wasn't hard to feel that he liked her there. The hard line of his erection jutted against her thigh, but his arms wound around her and he didn't seem at all bothered by the fact that he had a massive boner. He simply leaned back and started talking again.

"My mom and dad moved into town a few years back. They couldn't keep up so much land. They got a ton of money for it and they've been traveling ever since. They went to Iceland this year.

Why would anyone go to Iceland?"

"It's beautiful," she said. She'd seen it in a movie and it had been stunning. She was a girl who'd rarely been out of Texas. The idea of going somewhere so far away was like a dream to her. For so long, making rent had been her main goal. She'd never even thought about seeing the world. Now she wondered if that might be possible for her. Someday. "They probably wanted to see the northern lights."

"I think that was one of the items on their itinerary," he said, but now he was so close to her that he practically whispered the words in her ear, making her shudder, and not in distaste. "I'm sure I'll get to see pictures the next time I go home."

Being so close to Eric felt right. His arms were strong and warm around her, and it would be so easy to think for a moment that she was safe.

That would be a mistake.

"Deena, tell me why you went to Taggart today."

Shit. How the hell did he know about that? Maybe he didn't actually know anything. Maybe he was fishing. Rumors abounded at Top. The menu might change nightly, but the gossip was a mainstay. "I had to take him his lunch. He wasn't in the conference room. He's a weird guy."

Brazen her way through. It was the only thing to do. Act like nothing was wrong and it wasn't. She'd learned that a long time ago. As long as she had a smile on her face, people thought there was nothing going on under the surface and she never had to answer those uncomfortable questions.

"Did you read that part in the contract where you're not supposed to lie to me?" His voice was every bit as quiet as it had been a few moments before, but it had gone an icy cold that sent a chill along her spine. And the slightest bit of heat through her pussy.

She managed to nod. "I did and I talked to Master Ian about the program. That was all."

His mouth was right against her ear. "Are you sure that's all you want to say?"

She kind of wanted to see what he would do. Maybe that made her a brat, maybe it made her a bad submissive, but she was so curious. They were testing each other. That was what they were supposed to do, right? Test each other's boundaries. Get to know each other. She wanted to know how far Master Eric, the good and true knight to all females in trouble, might take this. "Yes, Sir. That's all I want to say."

He sat back. "I reserve the right to come back to this subject at a later date. We've only got a few minutes before the class is going to start and quite frankly, I would rather not admit that you need punishment on the second night of class. But don't think I'll forget."

Disappointment welled. She'd kind of wanted the connection. It seemed like spanking was the only way she was going to feel connected to this man, but she'd been right about him. He was a softie. That was a good thing because if he didn't give her what she needed, then she wouldn't be tempted by him. "What are we talking about tonight, Sir?"

It was best to get everything back on an even keel. He would forget any rumor he heard about her talking to Master Ian and then they could move on. If he kissed her again, she would deal with it. She might take it further or she might not. Whatever she did it would all be okay in the end because she was strong enough to walk away. She graduated from college a week after the training period was over and then she wouldn't even see him at work anymore because she already had a job lined up.

She looked up at him and he was watching as Masters Alex and Liam had begun to move into place.

"We're going to have our first class in how to use the equipment," Eric explained, his voice normal again. She studied the straight line of his jaw as he spoke. "There will likely be some kind of demonstration and then I would very much like to take you out for a cup of coffee and we can talk further."

So much talking. He seemed to seriously like to talk. How long had it been since she opened up and talked about anything? She rarely even mentioned how her day had gone beyond telling whoever had asked that it was fine. They would talk about the class and maybe he would tell her more about his childhood and how he ended up choosing the Navy and...

She wanted to know everything about him. A hundred questions popped up and she had to face the truth. That timer on their relationship might be the only thing that saved her from falling head over heels for this man. The training period would end and she could always walk away. She'd learned that lesson from childhood. When the going got tough, the tough moved on.

She cuddled against him because this part was nice. "That sounds good, Sir."

Maybe she would view this whole six weeks as a graduation present to herself. After that, it would be a whole new game and Eric Vail wouldn't even be a player.

Why did that make her so sad?

She let the thought go and concentrated on the lesson for the evening as Master Alex started to talk about impact play and all the fun toys associated with it. Yes, this was what she needed.

The rest didn't matter.

CHAPTER FIVE

"Hey, I thought I would find you in here."

Eric looked up from his brisket and smiled as Kyle Hawthorne strode in. Though he'd only made the decision to join the military a few weeks before, only told his mother last week, he already held himself with more pride than he had before. The young man who had seemed so sullen and withdrawn when he began to work at Top earlier in the year now walked into the kitchen with his shoulders straight, his head held high. "Kyle, you look good. You ready for OCS?"

Officer Candidate School. Unlike Eric, who had enlisted and gone to Great Lakes with the rest of the grunts, Kyle had a degree. It made more sense for him to train to be an officer. It also seemed to Eric to be proof that the kid was serious. He was heading to Newport in the morning.

Kyle grinned. "As ready as I can be." He sobered a bit. "I went out to the cemetery today. I know no one understands, but I was in that car with him. I have no idea why he died and I didn't. We were best friends for most of our lives and it doesn't make sense to me. I got out with a couple of scratches. I have to do something. I have to be better than I was before. My mother doesn't understand."

"I'm sure she understands more than you think she does. She's scared. You're her baby." He could remember his own mom crying when she'd found out, begging him to stay safe, while his dad had shaken his hand and told him how proud he was. "She's never going to be happy with you going off and putting yourself in danger, but she does know you need this. Why else would she be throwing this going away party?"

Kyle shook his head, his mouth turning up in a grin. "First, my mother loves a good party and second, I think she managed to totally piss Sean off. I heard that argument. I couldn't not hear it. People in Mexico might have heard it. Carys managed to sleep the sleep of the toddler dead, but I heard my mother blame Sean and the whole Taggart family for making this life seem glamorous."

Eric whistled. "Damn. How did that go over?"

Kyle leaned against the counter. "Have you ever heard a silence that was so loud you almost put your hands over your ears so you could pretend it wasn't happening?"

Sean had recently lost his brother to "this life." Eric could imagine Chef hadn't taken it well. "Are they all right now?"

Kyle nodded. "I think Mom realized what she'd said because they were quiet for a very long time and she was still clinging to him the next morning. Sean is a good man. I hate that I made them fight."

"We needed it," a feminine voice said. Grace was standing in the doorway. She wore a pretty emerald dress, her hair around her shoulders. Around her neck was a gold necklace with a heart attached. Eric had never seen her without it. It had taken him a while to figure out that was her collar, the gift from Dom to beloved submissive. "I haven't been talking to him because I've tried to give him space after what happened to Theo and let me tell you, saying what I said definitely got us talking. Sometimes you have to say the wrong things to get to the right outcome. Sean and I are fine, Kyle. And you couldn't possibly find a better role model than your stepfather and his brothers. I'm sorry you had to hear that, but I'm glad it's all out in the open and we can move on. Now, you should go out there because your stepdad has a present for you."

Kyle stopped and kissed his mother on the cheek before leaving the kitchen.

Grace remained behind. "You know you're supposed to be a guest tonight. I knew I should have fought Sean and had this whole thing catered in. I can't get you guys out of the kitchen. I've already hustled Cal and Mark out of here. They didn't think there was enough spice in the fondue dip. Macon was fussing with the cake earlier, and I swear Sebastian was crying over my taste in wines."

He put his hands up in defeat. The brisket was fine. His work here was done. He would have a talk with his line chefs about staying out of the boss's wife's appetizers. "Sorry. I'll get out of the way. I'll talk to the others."

Grace stepped in. "No, Eric, I'm the one who's sorry. About a whole lot of things. I haven't handled Kyle well. Or Sean. And I'm sure I haven't been very polite to you since I found out you're the one who talked Kyle into joining the Navy."

She'd been on edge. He wouldn't say she'd been impolite, but she hadn't been as friendly as she normally was. "Grace, it's fine. And I wouldn't say I talked him into it. He needed a place to go and I suggested he think about it. He's your son. I understand. My mom wasn't thrilled when I joined up, but I think we've all learned that bad things can happen at any moment. We have to hold on to what's good."

She nodded, her eyes going misty. "Yes, we have to stop looking at the past and hold on to what we have in the now and what good can come in the future. I'm glad he had someone who could guide him, and I would like to thank you for being so kind to my son."

"It was my pleasure. Your husband has been a hell of a mentor. There aren't many people who take a look at this mug of mine and hire me to be second in command, much less let me head up a second restaurant." In a world where chefs were celebrities, having the face of the restaurant be a scarred up vet wasn't ideal, but Sean didn't seem to care. He was making Eric a junior partner, giving him his own Fort Worth franchise of Top.

Eric was going to ask Deena to look over his business plans. He knew Sean had approved, but it might be nice to have a set of fresh eyes. Business was her major after all.

His sub was graduating from more than training class in a few weeks. He meant to give her something to do with her degree.

Grace gave him a hug and when she stepped back, she'd composed herself. "Well, I'm happy you're going to stay in the family. Don't think that Sean is being selfless by letting you open a second restaurant. He doesn't want to lose you and given how talented you are, someone was going to snap you up. Don't think he doesn't know about that drink you had with Tim Love three months ago."

He winced. He hadn't mentioned that to Chef because it hadn't meant anything. The culinary world was a small place. Tim was one of DFW's premiere chefs, but Eric was a loyal man. "It was only a drink, Grace. There was never serious talk about moving."

"And now there won't be. Go out and have a nice time. I saw Deena and Tiffany sitting and talking to Charlotte. She was giving them tips on how to handle their Doms."

If anything was guaranteed to give him the chills it was Deena taking advice from Charlotte Taggart. The woman wasn't averse to shooting people. "Yes, I should definitely handle that."

"Is everything going all right with you and Deena?" Grace asked before he'd made it out the door.

The last couple of weeks had been fun. Deena had proven to be every bit as curious as she'd told him she was. They'd played around with some bondage the night before. He had the most experience out of the training Doms so he'd been chosen to demonstrate some of the knots he knew. He'd gotten her down to her bra and wound his jute rope around her torso. He'd watched the way she responded, how she'd shivered, her eyes closing when his hands would caress her. She hadn't been afraid or wary then. She'd relaxed as he'd worked, and she'd seemed almost disappointed when he'd stopped. "It's going well. We're taking it slow."

He was giving her time. It was precisely why he hadn't punished her for lying to him about her conversation with Big Tag. He hadn't forgotten, but he was trying to be patient. If they were going to work, they couldn't run into the relationship without thought. Deena deserved a courtship. They'd had many classes together and after the last three they'd gone to a late night coffee shop and talked until he had to take her home because she had classes in the morning. She was finally talking to him about her childhood and what she wanted for the future. She'd told him about her father and how once he'd decided he was done with her mom, he'd been done with fatherhood, too. It was hard for Eric to imagine not knowing where his father was, but that was the reality Deena had faced at a young age.

Life had taught her that men couldn't be counted on. He intended to rewrite that lesson with one of his own.

The night before when he'd dropped her off, he'd walked her to her door and kissed her long and slow. When she offered for him to come in, he'd declined. He wanted it to be special for her. Hell, he wanted it to be special for him.

Grace studied him for a moment. "You've been dancing around each other for a year, Eric. How much slower can you possibly take it?"

"We've only recently started a relationship though. I think she needs time."

"And I'm fairly certain what that girl needs is crazy passion that sweeps her away." Grace looked over the dinner she was about to serve, making sure everything was warm. "Look, I've got some experience here. I was determined not to let Sean hook this pretty fish because I didn't trust that man as far as I could throw him, and that wasn't far. He was just as muscular back then. He was younger than me. He was hotter than me. I wasn't about to let that man into my bed much less my life."

"So what changed?" Deena had her reasons to keep distance between them. All the men in her life had failed her. It was why he'd let the lying thing go. He wouldn't do it again, but she'd been afraid of him and now he looked at that as a good thing. She would joke and laugh and pal around with most of the other male employees. In the beginning, he'd thought it was because she didn't like him, and now he realized she liked him too much.

"He walked into my backyard one night, jumped into my pool with his clothes on, and I've been his ever since," Grace said with a wistful smile on her face. "He overwhelmed me. Once he had me in his arms, I couldn't think about anything but him. All the reasons I couldn't allow him in kind of fell away and all that mattered was Sean."

He wasn't sure Grace and Deena had the same issues. Grace's husband had died. He hadn't abandoned her. Still, he understood what Grace was saying. He'd been hesitant to push their relationship past the boundaries of the club because he didn't want to scare her away. He wanted her trust before he moved them along, but the couples had been encouraged to talk outside of class. And he was different than the other trainees. The only reason he was going through training class was to acquaint himself with the club and how everything worked. If he'd had the money for a membership on his own, he would have applied and given his references and likely been accepted without training. As it was, he was being used more or less as a third instructor. He could start herding her gently toward a relationship outside the club. In a few weeks they would be asked to spend a couple of days under their training Doms' control as it was.

He nodded to Grace and began to make his way through her spacious home. He'd heard the story about how she and Chef had moved from Fort Worth to be closer to family when Carys was born. He walked through the halls, the walls dotted with pictures of the happy family. Smiling kids and loving couples. It reminded him of his own home in Missouri where his mom and dad had always kept pictures of him and Gwen, every one of their embarrassing school pictures on the wall for all to see.

He wanted that. He wanted the happy home and playful kids, and damn but he wanted that woman as his wife. Smart and sexy. Deena could light up a room when she smiled.

"Hey, did Grace kick you out of the kitchen?" Sean stepped away from the group he'd been talking to and held a hand out to Eric.

He shook Chef's hand, glancing over where Kyle was looking at his new tablet. "She did, indeed. It looks like he's happy with his new toy."

Sean nodded. "I've loaded it with every possible way for him to communicate with his mother. I know there will be times when he can't, but when he can I want him to have every opportunity. Are you looking for your girl?"

"Am I that obvious?"

Sean shrugged. "We're all that obvious. I saw her in the parlor. Come on. I'll take you there. I'm afraid she was talking to Charlotte. My sister-in-law loves to think of herself as a good influence on new submissives. She teaches them all the tricks to being a real brat."

"I was afraid of that." He followed Sean down the hall and heard Charlotte Taggart talking.

"Oh, I don't bother to manipulate Ian," the redhead was saying.

"His skull is far too thick. I've found direct confrontation is what turns him on."

Sean stopped before he rounded the corner. From here they could listen but not be seen. "Give it a minute and you'll understand what you're up against."

Yep, eavesdropping wasn't only for the line chefs. "I don't know that we should listen in."

"I have no idea what turns my Dom on," a familiar voice said. "It doesn't seem to be me."

Holy shit. That was Deena's voice.

Sean leaned in. "So we go in now?"

Bastard. "Not on your life."

How could she think she didn't turn him on? He got a hard-on anytime she walked into a room. She sat in his lap most of the time. She had to feel it. He'd worried at first that it might scare her off, but she hadn't said anything.

"I don't believe it." That was Tiffany. He would know her throaty voice anywhere. "That man is into you."

At least one of them had some sense.

He was very aware that he was standing outside the room like a teenager listening in. It was so far beneath his dignity, but every time he started to go in, Deena said something that stopped him in his tracks.

"If he is, then he has a funny way of showing it." Deena sounded very offhand, as though she couldn't care less. "Or maybe that's simply who he is. I knew it from the moment I met him. He's one of those guys. You know the type. Upstanding. Moral. Always doing the right thing."

There was a little laugh and then Charlotte said, "Sounds like a good man. You say it like it's a bad thing."

Yeah, he couldn't see how being upstanding was something to be sneered at.

There was a long sigh and then Deena spoke again. "There's nothing wrong with it. He'll make someone a great husband some day. It's just with that body and that gorgeous face of his, I expected a bad boy. I took one look at that man and thought he could rock my world. Then he opened his mouth and I realized he was a hearts and

84

flowers kind of guy. That would be awesome if I wanted that kind of relationship. I did the hearts and flowers thing. It got me divorced and with a mountain of debt. And zero orgasms. Like none. I've gotten better orgasms from a faulty vibrator than I ever got from that man's dick."

Sean snorted behind his hand. "Ah, the fairer sex. They're so genteel when it comes to intimacy. Let me warn you about something, Eric. The subs at Sanctum talk about sex way more than the Doms do."

He believed it. The Doms would sit around and talk about sports and the best place to find videos of dudes hurting themselves. They would never gossip about their sex lives. They would damn straight not complain that the sub they'd been assigned was too freaking nice to be sexy.

"I think he's trying to take it slow with you," Tiffany said, again proving she had more sense than his sub. "I think it's sweet."

"I've done everything I can to get that man to spank me again." He could practically see Deena shaking her dark hair.

"Did you try asking him?" Charlotte sounded harsher than before, as though she disapproved of what she'd heard.

There was a long pause. "I'm sorry. I shouldn't have done that, but I'm not sure how to ask a man to spank me. I was acting out and trying to get a reaction from Eric that I'm not going to get. At the end of this six weeks, I'll let Captain America find his perfect sub and I'll find my hot, dirty Dom. But I do get what you're saying. I'm trying to turn him into something he's not and I'll apologize to him."

Oh, yes she would. She would apologize very sweetly once he'd given her every fucking thing she wanted.

Eric nodded back toward the living room before turning on his heels and walking quietly down the hallway. Sean followed. When Eric was sure they couldn't be heard, he looked at Sean. "I'm going to need to leave a little early."

Sean shook his head as he fished around in his pocket. He came up with a key chain and quickly drew off a small gold key. "Nope. I think you handle that shit right here and right now. You mad?"

Angry? Not precisely. "I'm quite calm, but I'm very interested in showing my sub that she's wrong about a few areas of our relationship. She's got a safe word. I would never refuse to honor it. I don't think she'll use it. I actually think I'm falling into her trap and giving her everything she wants."

Sean grinned. "Oh, but sometimes traps can be fun. If you're serious about her, I would shut that bratty shit down now. Oh, she'll still try to manipulate you. Charlotte's high if she thinks she doesn't manipulate Ian."

"My skull's too thick to be manipulated," Big Tag said, walking up with what looked like a slice of lemon pie. "At least that's what my Charlie says when she's giving the newbies her talk. Damn, Vail, is she talking to your girl? Shut that shit down now. We went wrong when we decided to let the subs talk amongst themselves. Keep quiet. That's what I say."

Sean rolled his blue eyes. "Sure, you do. Your wife is the ringleader and that pie was supposed to be for dessert, asshole."

"Macon made two." Eric was not unaware of Big Tag's habit of stealing the desserts. He was always prepared—a fact Deena was about to learn the hard way. "I put one in the fridge for the big guy to find and the other in the…well, Macon knows where it is."

"It's in the beer fridge in the garage behind the wine bottles," Big Tag said. "Hey, dude, I do this for a living. And I left the second pie totally unmolested. Well, I might have licked it, but what are a few germs amongst friends?"

Sean looked back at Eric. "He's joking and don't bother trying to hide pies from him. He can find anything."

"That is unfortunately not true." Tag's smile dropped from his face and he seemed to lose his appetite, setting the pie on the table in the hall. "Should I go and talk to Charlie? If she's putting ideas in Deena's head, I'll talk to her about it."

"I'll take care of it. I was telling Sean I'm going to take my sub home and have a long discussion with her. I won't do anything that's not in our contract, but I am planning on using an implement you haven't signed me off on," Eric said honestly.

Ian waved him off. "I've talked to the patrons of the clubs you've been at before. You've been playing for a decade." That horrible guilt he'd seen slide across Big Tag's face seemed to lift for a moment. "Anything particularly dangerous?"

"Only to her asshole," he replied. He'd bought her a very nice plug yesterday. It looked like it was time for him to use it.

Big Tag slapped him on the shoulder. "Go forth and plug away, man. You know we've all turned into a bunch of pussies. We should plug our subs more often. And we should use the exotic lubes. A tiny bit of ginger, some jalapeño. That will get 'em moving. I'm going to have Grace put that on the calendar so I won't forget. It's important to keep up with the little things. Just because we've got two tiny humans who require our attention twenty-four seven doesn't mean that I shouldn't make time for an old-fashioned anal plugging. And why go home when you could use Sean's dungeon? Er, excuse me, the present room. He tells his kid that. Seriously, you're going to make her want to get in there even more than she normally would."

Sean handed over the key. "It's up the stairs, the last door on the right." He turned back to Ian. "I told her if she went into the present room, she wouldn't get any presents. That will keep her out of there. You know I've been doing this longer than you."

"I got double the kids, brother," Tag shot back. "I'm already more of a pro."

"Sure you are, asshole." Sean seemed to relish arguing with his brother. It was as though sarcasm was their own personal language. "And Eric, go on and set up and I'll send her to you in about ten minutes. You have your kit?"

"It's in my truck." He was a freaking BDSM Boy Scout and she was about to find that out.

She wanted a dirty Dom? He could give her one.

* * * *

Deena looked at Charlotte Taggart and wished she'd kept her damn mouth shut. Now the queen of the subs thought she was a brat. She kind of was. The last several weeks had been wonderful and frustrating all at the same time. She'd gotten to know Eric and it was as bad as she'd thought. He was practically perfect and the man could cook. She'd been out to his apartment for dinner on the night Top was closed. Naturally his apartment was neat and efficient, though she thought it was a bit bland. It needed some flair, but it was obvious the man took care of the place. He'd made her shrimp and grits and she'd nearly cried at how perfect they were. They'd laughed and talked and then he'd taken her home, walked her to her door and said good-bye.

The damn man hadn't even kissed her. He'd only kissed her twice since they'd agreed to be partners. She was starting to think he never would again.

"So your ex was an asshole?" Charlotte asked. At least she seemed to have moved on from that moment when Deena had admitted she'd been trying to get her ass spanked.

"Serious asshole," Tiffany said with a shake of her head.

That girl always had her back. "He dumped me, but only after I'd put him through law school." Why had she ever hidden this? It was freeing to be open about it. "He left me for one of the junior partners at the firm he hired on with after he graduated. He also left me with the beautiful gift of half his debt."

"Damn, I would have left him with a bullet to the balls," Charlotte said.

"Sometimes I wish I had," Deena replied with a sigh. "But it wasn't always bad. He was a good guy at one point. He was the kind of guy who opened doors and took care of a girl."

"No, that was his façade," Charlotte argued. The gorgeous redhead leaned forward. "He was never a good guy. No good guy could do what he did to you. You got fooled, Holmes. He played you."

"Yes, I guess he did." Somehow it seemed easier to believe he'd changed, that she hadn't been taken in so totally.

Charlotte's voice softened. "But that doesn't mean everyone's faking it. It doesn't mean there are no good guys in the world, and it definitely doesn't mean you need to be alone for the rest of your life."

"Who said I was going to be alone for the rest of my life?" They were venturing into dangerous territory. Maybe this was why she'd never talked about her past.

Tiffany raised her hand. She'd had more than a couple. Her cheeks were flushed a pretty pink from the rum punch Grace was serving. "That was me. Totally me."

She gave her friend a stare that she hoped would penetrate the rum haze she seemed to be in. "Is there a reason you talked about my private life to Big Tag's wife?"

Charlotte's eyes widened. "Oooo, you've got the intimidating stare down. Very nice."

Tiffany frowned. "I was worried about you. I think you're going to let something special go. I think you and Eric work and you're all 'I want to find some scumbag Dom who'll take me sexually and not care about me as a human being.'"

Wow, she was far gone. "Not once have I said those words. I have said I want to keep things casual and I would like to see what a bad boy can bring to the table, but that's my business and not yours."

"If she's your friend it's totally her business," Charlotte explained. "That's how friendship works. She can't turn off caring about you because you have boundaries. I've discovered that the best of friendships are also the ones where no one understands personal boundaries. A real friend will get all up in your business."

Which was why she avoided them, but looking at Tiffany she had to wonder what she'd cut herself off from. Tiff and Ally were her girls. And she hadn't hesitated to make her opinion plain when Ally had screwed up. She'd told Ally she'd fucked up and that she was mad but she still loved her friend.

Again, Big Tag's words seemed to float in, haunting her. Would she even call Ally and Tiff after she'd started her new job? Or would it be easier to let them go in favor of more superficial relationships?

"I'm scared of how much I feel for Eric," she admitted quietly.

Tiffany clapped her hands together. "I knew it. I knew you were madly in love with him."

"Not in love." She wasn't sure she had it in her anymore. Being in love was too much work, too much potential for disaster. "I like him. I care about him and I'm not sure how to ask for what I want."

Tiffany grinned. "You say 'hey, hot chef Dom, you should really tenderize this beef.'"

"She's going to need a ride home," Charlotte said. "Too bad her training Dom isn't here. As for you, you need to be honest with Eric. It's hard to openly talk about these things, but it's important. Intimacy and sex are things most of us view as private and dirty and taboo. We're so much happier as human beings when we acknowledge our needs and don't try to fight them because they're outside the norm.

He won't be shocked. He'll like the fact that you're talking to him."

"He'll definitely like the fact that she wants to have dirty sex with him," Tiffany said with another giggle.

Her friend was cutting loose tonight and it worried Deena a little. Tiffany wasn't the girl who got drunk at parties. She tended to be the one who looked after everyone else. If someone was going to make a scene at the boss's party, it would be Jenni.

Deena sighed. It looked like talking to Eric was going to have to wait. "I'll think about what you said, Charlotte. I better take this one home."

Tiffany's nose was a nice shade of red when she looked up at Deena. "I don't need to go home. I'm partying."

The very fact that she'd used the word "partying" gave Deena pause. Tiffany was a fun girl, but she didn't party or overdo anything. She was a serious artist, more thoughtful than wild. "We can party at your place."

She was going to feel like hell in the morning, and Deena wanted to be able to tell her friend that she hadn't done anything embarrassing in front of the boss.

"Deena, I need to speak with you for a moment," a deep voice said.

Shit. Tiffany might not be able to avoid the boss because Sean Taggart stepped into the room, and he seemed to be in full-on authoritative mode. His eyes were slightly narrowed, his shoulders squared off, and his voice deep. Was he pissed? "It's all right. I'm going to take her home."

"I don't know why we should go home. All the beer is here," Tiffany said, pushing her hair out of her face.

"I'll have someone take her home. I think Sebastian was planning on leaving soon. He'll take care of her," Sean said. "You have something else you need to do."

Sebastian seemed like a perfectly nice man, but Tiffany was her responsibility. "If you need me to help set up the buffet, I'm more than happy to do it, but she's my friend. I have to make sure she's all right."

Sean stepped up and looked down at her. "I admire that, Deena, but Sebastian can handle her. You have something else to do and it won't wait. Don't worry about Tiffany. Sebastian will treat her well. He doesn't put this out there often, but he's a trained Dom and I would trust him with Grace."

That was about as good a recommendation as Sean Taggart could give.

Tiffany managed to stand on wobbly feet. "I can take myself home."

"No, you can't," Deena shot back.

"Deena, I need you to go upstairs, last door on the right," Sean ordered in a tone that brooked no argument.

"Am I supposed to get something out of there?"

"Oh, you'll definitely get something." He put a hand on Tiffany's arm to help steady her. "Come on, Tiff. Let's get you home."

Charlotte watched as Sean eased Tiffany out of the room. There was a small smile on her face that Deena could only describe as mischievous.

"What's going on?" Deena asked, suspicion creeping in.

"Sometimes wishes get granted. Be careful though. Some wishes make our backsides ache." Charlotte winked and Deena was left standing in the middle of an empty parlor. She glanced toward the stairs. There was nothing else to do. It wasn't like she was going to walk away.

She started up the stairs and hoped curiosity was on her side.

CHAPTER SIX

Deena opened the door and felt her eyes widen immediately. Of all the things she'd expected to find, Eric standing there looking deliciously yummy without his shirt on wasn't it. She supposed she'd expected some sort of practical joke. The guys she worked with were good at those.

There was no humor in the way Eric was looking at her now. He stood in the middle of the room, right in front of…was that a spanking bench? She glanced around feeling somewhat like a mouse who'd walked right into a trap. She was in a private playroom. Chef's private playroom.

Why was she in Chef's private playroom with Eric? Her Dom. Her mind was starting to work overtime. Yep, she was in a private, beautifully done torture chamber with a man who had the right to punish her.

She stared for a moment, trying to grasp what the hell was going on. Eric was standing there, his shirt off, all those gorgeous muscles glistening. "Hi. Uhm, are you supposed to give me something to take down to the party? Chef told me to come up here. Is he doing a demo? I kind of thought this was a PG party, what with Grace's son being here and all."

He stepped forward, his bare feet moving over the hardwoods. She thought for a moment that he was moving toward her, but he stepped around her, passing her and moving to the door. She heard the door close and the snick of a lock being set into place.

"The party is certainly PG," he said, his voice a bit rough as he moved to stand in front of her. He was so tall. He towered over her, seemingly taking up all the space around them. "What goes on in here will be anything but. Now, Deena, it's far past time for us to have a long discussion about what happens to submissives who lie to their Doms."

"Lie?" She hadn't lied to him since those first couple of days. Well, mostly. She didn't tell him everything, but then he didn't need to know the things she didn't tell him. Maybe the best and easiest way out of all of this was to give him some truth in exchange. It was obvious to her that someone had talked about what happened last night. "I'm sorry. My stalker diner came in and he did try to grab my ass, but I handled him. It was fine."

His eyes flared and she realized she'd made a mistake. "He did what?"

"That wasn't what you were talking about?" She hadn't lied about anything else. Even that had been a lie by omission.

"No, but I'll add that to your punishment. I'm talking about the fact that you lied to me when you said you didn't go to Master Ian and request a new Dom for your training period. You sat there and looked at me and lied. You said you had gone in there to take him his lunch and that was all you talked about. I happen to know that isn't true. Unless you intend to tell me that Master Ian is the one who lied."

She was not even going to go there. A smart girl knew when she was caught. If she thought Eric could get a little spanky, she didn't even want to know what Master Ian would do to a sub who lied about him. The man had been an assassin at one point, if the rumors were true. "Nope. He did not lie. And I did take the man his lunch. I also had a very quick conversation with him about the possibility that you weren't the right training Dom for me, though I have changed my mind since then."

He stared down at her and if those gorgeous eyes of his had laser beams, she would have been dead then and there. "Don't try my patience, Deena. And don't think for a second that giving me big doe eyes is going to change my mind about punishing you. I told you that night I wouldn't forget and that punishment was coming. Here's the way this is going to go. You're going to take off your clothes. You're

93

going to fold them neatly because you have a party to attend afterward. You will then move to the mirror where you will lean over and grab your ankles, presenting your ass for my punishment."

"I'm going to do all those things? Any reason why I'm not using that very nice spanking bench?" Her voice was a little shaky, her hands already beginning a fine tremble because his voice was mesmerizing. This was not the happy, smiling Eric she was used to. This was not the man who held doors open for her and made sure she always locked herself inside her apartment before he would leave. This wasn't the man who made her a plate after work every night, always making certain she got the best of whatever they'd made.

This was the Dom and he wasn't a pushover.

"You are going to do everything I tell you to if you wish to continue as my submissive. And the spanking bench is a treat. I'm not giving you a treat, Deena. I'm punishing you for an infraction. Apparently for several. If you choose to forgo punishment, I'll explain to Master Ian that you're leaving the program and will need to move to the next training class where you will likely piss off another Dom."

Did he have to sound so certain of that? "Maybe the next Dom will be nicer than you."

His mouth flattened. "He won't. I'm as nice as it gets, baby, but I'm done being nice to you. It doesn't work. You don't want nice. You want me to spank you. You want a rough hand on your ass, getting your pussy nice and wet and ready for a long, hard fuck. That's where I might not be so nice to you. I might slap your ass, get you hot and horny, and then we'll spend the rest of the night with you serving me because there is absolutely nothing I want more than the feel of those lips wrapped around my dick."

Every word made her heart thump in her chest. This wasn't what she'd expected from Eric. She'd been certain he'd forgotten all about her teeny lie, but it appeared he'd merely been waiting for the right moment to pounce.

He wanted to feel her lips around his cock? They'd fallen into a comfortable friendship. Was she ready to try something more with this man?

"Or you can be a total coward and walk out of here and never know if it could have worked between us," he continued. "You can scamper off and I won't come after you again because I'm through playing this game by your rules. If you do stay in this room with me, our relationship changes. No more training wheels. For as long as our contract lasts, you'll be mine and I will take you when I want you, how I want you, wherever the hell I want you, and no one is going to come between me and my sub. You'll be mine to take care of, to pleasure when you're good and punish when you deserve it. If you choose not to even try to make it work, you'll have to watch me with someone else because I am ready. I'm ready to not be alone. I'm ready to find some pleasure in life, and if you won't have me, then I'll find someone who will. I'll find a woman who will take this ugly mug of mine in exchange for taking care of her in a way only I can. A woman who wants the pleasure and pain I can give her, the safety I can offer."

"Don't you ever say that again." She hated it when he talked that way. Her hands were trembling again as she stepped close to him and put her palm against the scar that ran over the side of his face. "You are not ugly. Don't even pretend."

He softened, but only slightly. His hand came up, holding her palm to his face. "You're the one I want, Deena, but you need to understand that I won't wait forever. I want you to want me, too, but if you can't, I will move on. Make your decision."

He let go and stepped back, giving her space. That was what he'd been doing all this time. She'd thought they were falling into friendship and all along he'd been the wolf in sheep's clothing waiting for the right moment to pounce.

He was too much, too scary for her to even think about staying with. If she couldn't handle her ex, she was sure she wouldn't be able to handle Eric.

But she couldn't force herself to move. She needed to back away and protect herself, but a sudden vision of Eric with another woman nearly brought her to her knees. As though they moved of their own volition, her hands came up, fingers unbuttoning the blouse she wore. Her eyes locked with Eric's, and she saw the moment he realized she wasn't walking away. Those green orbs flared and then satisfaction settled over him. His sensual lips curled up as he watched her undress.

95

She was so aware of what she was doing. This was what had been missing before when it came to sex. The lovers she'd taken had been hurried and thoughtless, more concerned with pleasure than real intimacy. Eric was forcing her to take her time, to connect with him. It was scary, but she couldn't stop herself. She wanted the connection with him. He was right. If she walked away without even trying, she would regret it.

Her ex had taken something from her. It was far past time to see if she could get it back. This piece of herself, the sexual self she'd never explored, had lain dormant. It had been sent into hiding by cruel words and self-doubt, and she could feel it stirring under Master Eric's hot gaze.

He hadn't been lying. He wanted her. He wanted to do all those nasty things he'd promised and she worried he would follow through on every one of them. The Dom was definitely in charge tonight.

She slipped her fingers under the front clasp of her bra, unhooking it and feeling her nipples rasp against the cotton cups. Her ex had told her she needed to get into better shape, but she'd always liked her body. It was curvy and soft, but strong. Somehow she knew Eric would like it, too. Though she was seeing a rougher side of the man, she knew deep down he was still Eric. He could talk a filthy game, but there wasn't an unkind streak in the man. She eased the bra off and folded it, laying it and her blouse in his waiting hands.

"Now the jeans. Leave your shoes by the door."

She started to unbutton the fly of her jeans and felt the waistband of her undies. Yeah, she wasn't supposed to wear those. She rapidly calculated the likelihood of slipping them off with her jeans and getting away with it. Not good odds. "Uhm, Sir, I didn't realize we were playing tonight."

"Are you serious?" His eyes narrowed. "Tell me you didn't disobey a direct order. Tell me you're not wearing panties."

"I would love to be able to do that, but jeans are rough on a girl's hoo haw."

"Do you know what else is rough on your pussy? A violet wand. Maybe a TENS unit. Do I have to attach an electrode to your private parts to remind you of what the rules are? Or should I spank that pussy raw? Is that what you want?"

She wasn't sure why, but when he talked like that her whole body seemed to go limp and submissive. "No, Sir. I'm sorry, Sir. I didn't think we would be playing tonight. You haven't wanted to play outside the club."

He got into her space again, taking her chin with his left hand and forcing her head up so she had to look at him. "You don't guess at what I want or what I don't want. I told you what would happen if I caught you in panties again so you will not be getting these back and when I take you home tonight, you will surrender the rest of your underwear to me. I will decide if and when you get them back. You signed a contract that made your body mine. I've been indulgent up to this point, but you keep pushing me. If you're not careful, I'll be selecting every item of clothing you are allowed to wear outside of work. Do you want that, Deena? Do you want me to make those decisions for you? Do you want to give up that much control?"

She shook her head. That idea held no appeal at all. She liked the idea of being submissive for sex and play, but she was too independent to go any further. "No, Sir. I won't wear them when we're together."

"Give them to me."

She hurried to do his bidding, the whole place seeming to shrink. She knew the house she was in was huge and filled with people, but the world seemed to shrink down to the two of them. She could no longer hear the sounds of the party. Only his voice mattered. She shoved out of her pants, dragging her panties with them. She folded the jeans, placing the black cotton undies on top. She wouldn't be seeing them again. She was going to miss wearing underwear, but it would be worth it to keep her body feeling so alive and ready. Her skin was tingling, waiting for the moment he would lay those big, callused hands on her.

Eric nodded toward the mirror that ran the length of one side of the room. She turned and there she was in all her glory. No way to miss that. She was so naked, her nipples taut and skin flushed with arousal.

"Yes, I want to stare, too. You're as fucking gorgeous as I thought you would be, and you have no idea how many times I managed to picture you naked. I didn't even come close to the real thing." He stood behind her, so close she could feel the heat rolling off his body. "Tell me I can touch you. I know it's in our contract, but I want to hear you say it. I want to know you're doing this because you want me, not just because we have a contract between us."

He needed reassurance. Somehow it made the encounter sweeter. He'd given her all the dirty words she needed to get hot and to feel like she was sexy and lovely. It was easy to forget he needed the same. He was a man and he needed to know he was wanted. Alarm bells went off in her head, but they seemed distant now.

She locked eyes with him in the mirror. "I want you, Eric. It's not about the contract, though I like the contract. I want to see where you can take me. I'm scared. Not of the pain. Not of the punishment."

"You're scared of the emotion between us." He brushed the hair off her shoulder and planted a kiss on the nape of her neck. "I've always known that, but it's going to be all right, Deena. We'll go slow in that department. But not in the rest of it. It's time to move forward with our D/s relationship. Go and do as I asked."

He was going to do it. He was going to smack her ass and then…she wasn't sure what he would do then. He might touch her. He might demand that she get to her knees and service him with her mouth. He might give in and give her his cock.

It was so easy now that she was here. She'd agonized for weeks over what she wanted, but now it was clear. She wanted a sexual relationship with this man. She wanted to experience what it truly meant to be Eric Vail's submissive.

Deena stepped across the space toward the mirror, the wood at her feet slightly chilly. The air was chilled as well, but she didn't mind. It was one more sensation to be had, one more bit of proof that she was alive. She felt it now—how alive she was. Too often she moved through her days with the only thought being to get through to the next one. He was forcing her to focus on the now.

She took a deep breath and bent over, grasping her ankles. Her body stretched, the sensation pleasurable as her muscles released.

A smack filled the air and then she felt a sting of pain. He'd slapped her ass with what was very likely a crop. Had he come prepared for the evening? As he'd driven her here, talking about innocuous things, had he been thinking of doing this to her?

"Spread those legs farther apart. When I tell you to assume the position, I want your feet shoulder width apart and your ass in the air."

"Yes, Sir." She moved her legs apart, her vulnerability becoming increasingly evident. In this position, he would have access to her backside and her pussy. He could likely see her pussy through the part in her legs.

The crop caressed her skin, the leather tip moving over her ass cheeks. "That's what I want to hear, baby. But do you honestly think that all this sweet submission is going to save you? Do you think if you give me a breathy little 'yes, Sir,' that I'm going to be satisfied?"

She knew exactly how to answer that one. "No, Sir."

"I don't know about that. I think you think I'm a pussy Dom."

Shit. That was not a good thing for a sub to think about her Dom. Even though she kind of had thought it, she didn't want him to think she'd thought it. "Not at all."

The crop came down, smacking her hard and making her eyes water. "I think you do. I think you tell all your friends how easy I am, how I let you get away with anything you want. You might even tell them how you manipulate me."

Another hard blow and she shook her head, careful not to let loose her grip on her ankles. Had he been listening in when she'd been talking to Charlotte? "It was only talk, Sir."

Three more swats and she whimpered, the pain flaring hard and then turning into heat along her flesh.

"I think you meant every word of it, baby." He knelt down beside her, his fingers brushing off a tear that she'd squeezed out. "I think it's time to give you something else to talk about. The next time you have a discussion with your friends about your Dom, I want you to tell them about this. It's twenty for lying to me about talking to Master Ian. Another twenty for disobeying my directive about wearing panties. Then I think I have to be a bit more extreme when it comes to allowing a man to molest you at work without telling me or allowing me the right to protect you."

"It wasn't a big deal, Sir." She'd handled him. He very likely wouldn't be back.

He moved quickly, his hand coming up to find her nipple. He

twisted it between his thumb and forefinger, the pain nearly making her cry out. "Don't make this worse. If he ever walks in again, you will come and get me. You will refuse to serve him and I will have a long talk with the asshole. It is my responsibility and my right to protect you. Don't you take that away from me. If all you expect from a Dom is play and pain, then I'm not the Dom for you. I want to be meaningful to you. And if some woman tries the same with me, I fully intend to sic you on her, so if you can't protect me, you should tell me now."

It was the exact right thing to say and she had to smile. It proved he knew she wasn't a burden. She could be a partner. "I'll take her down, Sir."

"I know you will. I also know you're going to enjoy the next few minutes so I don't require a count. What happens afterward is going to be a bit unpleasant, so I suggest you enjoy your spanking." He stood up with those enigmatic words and then fire rained down on her ass.

She lost count of how many times the crop came down. She would hear that zippy sound and then the slap of leather hitting skin before the pain registered. Heat sank into her skin, making her whimper and moan, but she didn't want him to stop. She could already feel the adrenaline and endorphins kicking in as he worked her over. Just the right amount. Too much and the pain overruled the pleasure. Too much and the rush would be lost in a haze of ache. Naturally Eric knew what he was doing. It was like watching the man cook. He always knew exactly how long to cook a dish to make it utter perfection. With every stroke of his crop he proved to be a master at this, too. The pain would flare, tricking her mind, and then heat would settle in, making her body flush and alive.

She held on, riding the storm he created. Her body was trembling, but she wasn't about to move, wouldn't cry out and tell him she needed him to stop because she didn't. She wanted this glorious symphony of pain and pleasure and connection. Every now and then she would feel his free hand on her. He would pause for a moment and run his fingers along her spine as though ensuring himself she was all right. Then the process would begin again.

Tears dripped from her eyes making the world seem hazy and

unreal. She didn't have to be everyday Deena in this place. She didn't have to worry about school or how she was going to make the rent. In this place, there were no mistakes to regret. There was only the crop and the sound of her Master's voice.

"Do you have any idea how beautiful you are right now?" The crop slapped against her, a rhythm she was sure her heart beat to. "Your skin is perfectly pink and that pussy is pouting, begging for my attention."

She was sure it was since she could practically feel the damn thing pulsing. Sex had always been about her partner, a way to show her partner how much she cared, but now it seemed like more. It seemed like a need, a desperate need to connect with this one man, and not only for his sake. She wanted. For the first time in her life, she craved a man's cock. If he didn't take her, she might cry because she was already close to something wonderful, something that had eluded her before.

"That was forty, baby," he said, his hand still on her backside.

"It's already over?" She didn't want it to be. She might stand there all night, allowing him to make her ass red, if she could only stay in this place.

"Unfortunately, yes, but we're not through. You've paid for the lying and the disobedience." His hand moved over her tender backside and slid down to hover on the edge of her pussy. "Now we're going to have a discussion about what will happen if that man walks in and you don't tell me. But first I want to know if you liked my discipline. Tell me, Deena, how does your pussy feel?"

The question was too intimate, but somehow in the quiet of the playroom, it was all right to open up to him. "Hot. Aching. Needy."

"You're wet, baby. Look at that." His words were sultry, his voice a sexy groan as he slid a finger through her pussy.

She'd been perfectly still while he'd smacked her ass, but her whole body shook now. She wanted that finger inside her, thrusting in and out.

A hard hand came down on her ass, making her yelp because she was so damn sensitive there.

"Did I give you permission to move?" Eric asked the question in a low growl, the sound sizzling along her skin.

He seemed intent on playing the hard-ass. She was never going to let that man know she thought he was a little soft again. He overcompensated.

Or he was simply the yummiest mix of badass Dom and sweet as pie man she'd ever met—a completely dangerous combination because she still wasn't sure she was ready for what he wanted outside the playroom. She shoved all those thoughts aside. They didn't have a place here. There was no future and no past in this room. There was only the glorious now, where she had a Dom to please.

"No, Sir." She stilled, though her back was starting to ache.

His big palm moved along her spine. "Come on then, baby. You've been in that position forever. Let's stretch you out. In more ways than one."

She wasn't sure what he meant with the second remark, but she sighed in relief as he helped her straighten up. Every muscle in her body stretched deliciously, and she could feel the hot ache in her ass. "Thank you, Sir."

He was standing right in front of her, his big body invading her space. His bare chest brushed against hers and that restless feeling started up again. She needed more than mere punishment from this man. His hands slid down her body to her hips. "Tell me how you're feeling."

Some subs would wait until their Doms gave them permission to touch them, but she couldn't see that coming from Eric. He might have been rough with her backside, but he wouldn't put that wall between them. She brought her hands up to finally feel that magnificent chest of his. Warm, smooth skin covered his muscles, and she could see him sigh in pleasure at the contact. "I feel good, Sir. I feel happy and warm, but I definitely don't want to stop playing with you."

He brought his forehead down to meet hers. "You're not worried about what I'm going to do next?"

She ran her hands across his deltoids and up to those broad shoulders. "I'm sure it will be suitably horrible, Sir, and no, I'm not worried."

"Because I'm the pussy Dom?"

She tilted her head up. "No, because you're Eric."

His hands moved up, sinking into her hair. His lips took hers and for the first time in a long time, she felt like she'd gotten something right.

* * * *

Sometimes it sucked to be the Dom. He brought his mouth down on hers, letting his lips move and play. All he wanted to do was sink his aching cock inside her and spend the rest of the night making her scream. Her tongue slid against his as her hands moved all over his torso. She was exploring him and he didn't want that to stop, but he had a freaking point to make with her and they were both going to get punished.

It was the way she'd said "because you're Eric" that had done him in. For a moment before she'd responded, his heart had taken a dive. She wanted a bad boy and he hadn't proven it to her. The spanking he'd given her wasn't the worst, but he didn't want to go much further. If she needed more of a sadist, she would have to find someone else. He preferred to be the indulgent Master, lavishing his sub with affection and pleasure in exchange for her offering him her body and trust.

Of all the things she'd done, leaving him out of the situation with the handsy diner was the one he hated the most. He needed to be needed. He craved it. Even from his friends, he wanted to be the one they called when they needed a hand. It was something that had been bred into him by his parents, or perhaps he'd simply been born that way, but the idea of a woman he cared for, one he was responsible for, being in trouble and not calling him made him ache inside.

So his cock had to wait.

He broke off the kiss, though he didn't push her away yet. He loved the silky feel of her naked body against his. The woman should never wear clothes. She was soft and feminine and so fuckable, he was going to die if he didn't get inside her soon. He'd thought it was rough before. He'd thought waiting and being patient had been a trial. Now that he knew what she looked like, how wet her pussy could get, how her nipples felt against his chest…this was a special ring of hell.

"Go on, baby. Go to the spanking bench and find a comfortable position. I need access to your ass."

Her face tilted up and her eyes widened. He could never let her know how those eyes kicked him in the gut every time she looked at him with that innocent stare of hers. "More spanking?"

She would like that. Despite being a newbie, she had a nice threshold for pain. He was certain she'd found a happy, floaty place while he'd worked her over. "No and don't question me again. Go."

She turned and he watched as she scurried over to the spanking bench. That woman jiggled in all the right places. Damn, but he wanted her. There was no reason he shouldn't have her after he'd done his very best to remind her of the rules.

He watched as she settled herself awkwardly onto the bench before moving back to where he'd lain out everything he would need. While Sean had taken his time sending Deena up, Eric had prepped for their play. He found it soothing to wash and prep all the toys he'd purchased for her. Especially the very nice butt plug she was about to become acquainted with. Yes, he was going to enjoy this. Patience was the better way to go.

She would require all of this because even though she was submitting so very nicely tonight, he knew the battle wasn't over. She might have accepted him as her Dom for the time being, but she had demons he was going to have to battle to get her to accept him as more than a lover.

He moved carefully, taking his time despite the ache in his groin. He was well aware she would have welcomed him a few moments before. If he'd pressed her, she would have spread her legs and allowed him inside her, but he needed more from her, needed to teach her that she wasn't a casual lay to him. She was everything. He unrolled the small anal plug. He picked up the lube and strode back over to her.

"Sweetheart, have you ever taken a plug before?" He knew the answer, but he wanted to see her reaction.

"What?" She nearly came off the bench.

He put a hand on her back, keeping her down. Yes, that had been priceless. Maybe he was more of a sadist than he thought. He'd adjusted the bench to the height he wanted her at. Her pink ass was up in the air, her pussy on display as well. She'd settled her legs and arms on the rests and her generous breasts hung from either side of the bench. All her pretty parts ready for him to play. "Do I need to tie you down?"

He felt a shudder go through her.

"I can be still. I don't know about the plug thing though."

"Baby, how am I ever going to fuck your tiny little asshole if we don't open you up a bit? You said you were open to anal sex. This is the first step. You'll accept my plug and you'll wear it for the rest of the party. You won't take it out until I drive you home and take it out for you. For the next couple of weeks, you'll wear it for several hours a day. I'll move you up in size until you can handle my cock."

"But what about work days?"

"It's fine because I'll pick you up on the days we work together and you can work your shift with a plug in your ass. When the shift is done, I'll remove it and reward you. For every day you successfully keep the plug in, you get to pick your treat. Whether it's a dinner you want me to cook, a task you need me to provide, or if you want me to eat your pussy until you scream, that's what you'll get."

It was all a part of slowly moving into her life. He would make it a game. She wouldn't see how necessary he'd become until it was too late. He had to be sneaky with her.

"If I take the plug, which I am terribly afraid of right now, will you make…will you have sex with me?"

Oh, she'd gotten it right the first time, but he wasn't going to play semantics with her. "If you think for a second that you're leaving this room without taking my cock, you don't understand how much I want you. Every second I'm not inside you is pure hell."

She seemed to settle down. Yes, she was so very afraid. Manipulative brat. "I do trust you. And I do want you, Eric. Sir. It's been a very long time for me and I'll be honest, sex wasn't something I was good at before. Maybe the plug will make the difference. Maybe all I needed was a piece of lubed-up plastic shoved up my butthole. I don't know, but I'm willing to give it a shot."

"I'm so glad to hear it." He couldn't help the smile that slid across his face. The woman made him laugh. It was one of the first things he'd noticed about her. He smiled so much more when she was around. "This is going to be a bit cold."

And then it would get hot. So hot, he wasn't sure he'd ever get over it, but then he didn't want to. He wanted to be in her heat for the rest of his life.

He parted her cheeks and took a moment to stare at her. She was lovely and this was so intimate. She'd been married before, but he would bet no one had ever seen her like this. She'd never been so soft and vulnerable and trusting with anyone except him.

The air around them was quiet. He was fairly certain Sean had the whole room soundproofed. It was a smart bet since he and Grace had a kid. He'd spied a baby monitor, which he'd made certain wasn't on. The playroom was quiet and intimate, a space for lovers to lock out the rest of the world and concentrate on one another.

He was concentrating on all her pretty girl parts. He lubed up the plug and placed it against her tight hole. "Relax for me. This won't hurt. It's only a little uncomfortable."

He rimmed her gently, circling her with the tip of the plug.

Her breath came out in sporadic huffs. "Oh, you know so much about this, do you? How many times have you gotten plugged?"

How little she knew. He pressed the plug in and pulled it back out, gaining ground with each twist and turn. "Unlike you sweet subs, the Doms had already been through a four-week course before we were even allowed to meet you, and we were forced to endure everything we want to be able to do to you. If you want the right to spank a sub at Club Sanctum, you have to be able to handle one, and let me tell you those Doms don't play around. Well, actually they do. They make bets on whether they can get us to cry or say our safe words. Assholes. Did I mention you have a very beautiful asshole?"

A choking sound hit his ears and Deena's spine quivered. It was good to know he could make her laugh, too. "No, you had not mentioned that. I'm very flattered. I try to keep it tight down there. Please tell me Big Tag plugged you. Wow, that feels weird."

He would give her a bit of a need for revenge. After all, he happened to know that it did feel pretty weird. She was obviously doing her best to remain perfectly still. He worked the plug over and around, pressing in deeper and deeper. There wasn't a ton of pain when a plug was applied with the proper amount of lube, but the full sensation hadn't been too bad. "I'm sorry to disappoint. They made us practice on each other. Let me just say that your friend Althea does not have a gentle hand."

Her laughter rang through the room.

He looked down at his handiwork. There was now a small pink plug in her backside, nestled there, and she hadn't even realized it was done. He did have a gentle hand. "You're plugged, baby."

"I am?" Her head came off the bench as though she could look behind her and see what was going on. "That wasn't so bad. None of it was." She seemed to realize her mistake. "I mean, I barely survived, Sir, and I will always remember the lessons taught here tonight."

She was going to give him so much trouble. He stepped away, quickly washing his hands and getting that other bit of equipment he needed. "What makes you think the lessons are through? I believe we talked about moving this relationship forward. I haven't finished yet."

He stepped back to her. This wasn't how he wanted to make love to her the first time. He wanted to do it in a bed when they had hours and hours to explore and play, where he could show her how he really felt, but that would lead to her running away as fast as she could. She wanted a bad boy to fulfill her fantasies. He needed to show her he could be everything she wanted. He needed to prove to her it was safe to let herself care about him, and he wasn't going to do that by scaring her away. If dirty, filthy, glorious sex was what would reel his prize in, then he would have to go for it.

And he was playing the big bad Dom. He didn't have to play polite. He stepped in front of her. She was still soft and submissive on the bench, her head turned to one side. Her mouth wasn't exactly where he needed it, but he could make due. "Do you know what game we're going to play now, baby?"

She licked along her bottom lip and her cheeks flushed. "I don't know, Sir."

He showed her the condom wrapper. "I'm going to put this right here." He laid it on the curve of her ass. "It needs to stay here. If it falls off, we'll have to start all over again, and I do mean all over again. More spanking, and this time with a plug in your ass. If you lose the plug, well, I'll have to assume you want a bigger one."

"You're mean." She breathed the words out, but he could see the twinkle in her eye. "So I'm supposed to lay here? For how long?"

She didn't realize how mean he could be. His hands went to the button of his fly and he shoved down his jeans and boxers. His girl was right about denim being hell on a person's undercarriage. She was going to have to switch to skirts from now on. "You'll have something to do. I wouldn't want you to be bored."

With a sigh of relief, he unleashed his dick. He was rock hard and wanting, but he was so close to getting some relief. He hadn't dated since the day he'd met her, hadn't wanted another woman, so it had been a long dry spell for him.

Her eyes widened. "Wow. That is probably way bigger than the plug thingee, Eric."

He stroked himself, satisfied with the way her breathing had picked up. "Yes, but you'll be ready for it. Would I hurt you?"

He hoped she at least understood that much.

"No, you wouldn't mean to." Her hands curled over the sides of the bench. "I'm going to win this game, Sir. Do I get a prize?"

His balls were already drawn up against his body. He wasn't sure she needed to do anything but turn that sultry voice on him to get him to go off like a rocket. He definitely needed a good recipe with a ton of ingredients to get through this. Something complex, with spice and substance, rather like the woman herself. "Lick the head. I want to feel your tongue on me. Be careful though. Any movement of your pretty ass could make that condom fall, and you don't want your Dom to have to pick it up."

"No. I don't want to start all over again," she said, her eyes on his cock. "I want to win."

He hated that she turned it into a competition, but he needed time to make her see that while this was a game, she would always win. Life hadn't taught her that lesson. He was going to have to be patient, but thank god at least the waiting to have her would be over soon.

Then he felt the warmth of her tongue drag across his cock, and he wasn't thinking about anything else.

Except how to stop himself from coming like a fifteen-year-old virgin. Deena sucked the head of his cock into her mouth and then he was desperate to find something else to think about other than how fucking good that felt.

He could go classic. *Pâté de Canard en Croûte*. It was a recipe made famous by Julia Child that every chef had to figure out at some point in time or another.

She whirled her tongue around his cock as she managed to take him deeper without shifting her backside. She was determined and obviously willing to do whatever it took to win this particular game.

Five pound duck. Half a teaspoon of salt. An eighth of pepper. She found the slit in his cockhead and ran the tip of her tongue over it. *Pinch of allspice. Two tablespoons Cognac.* His cock was straining as she worked her mouth over and around.

Later, he would be able to take his time. He would learn her body better than he knew his own. He would thrust in and out of her mouth until she couldn't handle it anymore, and then and only then would he give in and take her pussy.

Two tablespoons of port. What else? He couldn't think of it, couldn't think of anything else. If he didn't pull out of her hot mouth, he was going to fill her and he wasn't through yet.

"Stop." He pulled out, tugging lightly on her hair.

Her lips curled up like the cat who'd managed to get all the cream. That condom hadn't moved. Not a centimeter. He groaned as he ripped the package open and managed to get the damn thing on his cock. He wasn't playing it cool, wasn't being the Dom he wanted to be, but there was nothing else to do now. He wasn't about to step away and leave her aching. It wasn't in him.

He moved in behind her, gently lifting her hips so he could line himself up before wetting his cock in the slick moisture of her pussy. If anything, she'd gotten hotter than she'd been before. His girl seemed to enjoy the game they'd played. Or perhaps what she enjoyed was his undivided attention and appreciation.

"Yes, baby, I can't wait a second longer to have you. I tried every mental trick I know to put it off, but your mouth felt too good to resist." Her husband obviously hadn't given her enough love. She didn't understand her own value. Deena had no idea how sexy and amazing she was. He could fix that. He wouldn't ever get tired of telling her how beautiful she was. "I'm not going to last. I want you too much."

She settled against the bench. "It's okay. I've had fun."

Did she think he was going to take what he wanted and give her nothing back? "Oh, fun is not all you're going to have."

He pressed in, her tight clasp nearly unmanning him, but now he had a challenge to face. She wasn't getting off this bench until she'd screamed out his name. By the time he was done, she would know exactly how much he could offer her.

She was tight, but he was ruthless. Pressing in, he could feel not only how hard her pussy clamped down on him, but also the crazy drag of the plug against his cock.

"I'm so full. I almost can't stand it. Almost," she said, her chest moving as she dragged air into her lungs. Her hands were fisted on the handles.

"You can take it. You can take every inch of me." He pulled on her hips, forcing another inch in. He angled up, not able to take his eyes off the place where his cock was sinking in, joining them for the first time. "You were built to take me."

He let his right hand slip around to find her clitoris. The plump button was slick and ready.

Deena gasped, her body bucking under him.

Neither one of them was going to last, but that was all right. This was only the first time. There would be so much more. He still had weeks to show her how good they could be together. Quick and hard or slow and easy, they would make love in every way possible until she couldn't imagine not being with him.

He thrust in and pulled back out, finding a rhythm. He pounded into her, absolutely certain she was with him. Her back bowed as she tried to thrust back, fight for her own pleasure.

"Eric, I don't…" She seemed to have forgotten to call him Sir, but he reveled in it. In the quiet moments, the most intimate ones, he wanted to be Eric, her lover, her protector, someday so much more.

"Let it happen. Let go, baby. I'll catch you." He pressed down on her clit as he stroked inside. "This is the way it's supposed to be between us. This is what happens when it's right."

She screamed out his name and he let go, bucking into her, giving up everything he had. The orgasm washed over him like a wave crashing and he rode it. His body came alive, pumping into her.

Finally, when he had nothing left to give, he stopped, putting a hand on her back. He could feel her trembling in the aftermath. "Are you all right, baby?"

"I'm…I'm good. It's fine." She was quiet and he could almost see her withdrawing.

Too much. Too much emotion. Too much connection. If he pushed her too hard, he would lose her.

It was time to play the bad boy again. He bent over and kissed the small of her back, one last affection before he too withdrew.

When he stood up again, he smacked her ass hard enough to jar that plug inside her and make her jangly and achy all over again.

"You did well, but don't forget for a second that I was in control. I won't be so easy on you next time." He slid the condom off, tied it and threw it away before washing his hands again. He had a brisket to serve. Cooking and sex. His two favorite things and all in one night. He intended it to be routine after tonight.

"My bottom is sore and there's a plug in it, so I wouldn't say you were so easy, Sir." The sass was back in her voice.

He would let her hide for a little while longer. "Wash up and get dressed then come downstairs. You'll be by my side for the rest of the evening."

Her head came up, a frown on that pretty face as he tugged his shirt over his head and slipped into his boots. "Uhm, shouldn't you help me up and treat me like a princess?"

"Baby, I did. My princess likes orgasms." He kissed the top of her head, well aware of what her real problem was. "Don't you dare lose that plug."

"Eric, how am I supposed to get off this thing without losing the plug?"

Yeah, he totally had a sadistic side. He patted her pretty ass. "You're a smart girl. I have faith in you. Five minutes, Deena, or I'll send someone up to get you. And never, ever forget that I can be a bad boy and a good man."

"You're not being a very good man right now," she groused.

He couldn't help the grin that came over his face. "You never know what you'll get, baby. See you in a few."

As he closed the door, he could have sworn he heard her laughing.

CHAPTER SEVEN

Eric stared out the front window of his truck. His pretty sub was a definite distraction, but Dallas traffic required all of his attention. "I said it's puppy play night."

Deena turned in her seat. He'd come to think of it as hers since she spent so much time in it. Way more time than anyone else had ever spent. He picked her up and drove her home every day from work and then again to the club during training classes. Often he would come inside and work the plug into her backside before taking her hard and fast.

They still hadn't done it in a damn bed. She seemed to like the fervent, D/s oriented sex. He was getting too old to fuck standing up. He wanted more. He wanted to get her in bed and take his time, getting his mouth on her. Yeah, he hadn't done that yet, either. Every time they started moving toward serious intimacy, she would pull away and he would end up going home frustrated as hell.

"I'm not sure about puppy play night," she said.

"Really? Because you put it down as something you were interested in." He hadn't mentioned it to her because she'd marked it on her contract, checking the yes box with the same blue check she'd used on bondage, suspension play, and impact play.

She crossed her arms over her chest, staring out the front window as he inched forward. Silence came from her side of the car.

"Baby, did you think you would literally be playing with

puppies?" She'd been a newbie coming into the training program, all of her knowledge having come from books she'd read, and not nonfiction. Though she'd been given a list of nonfiction to read, now he wondered if she'd bothered or thought that Amber Rose's romance novels covered it all. They apparently hadn't covered puppy play, which did not involve actual puppies. Or she was freakier than he'd ever imagined. "Baby, you didn't think we were going to do something sexual with small dogs. Please tell me that's not true."

They were stopped on the freeway, so he managed to get a glimpse of her flushing.

"Don't be nasty. I never thought that. I hadn't heard of it before the class and it sounded like it would be fun. I thought maybe it was like a bonding experience for subs. Now that someone explained it to me it sounds weird, and I am not peeing on a fire hydrant for you."

He burst into laughter at the very thought. She always went to the extreme. It was one of the things he'd discovered about her over the weeks they'd been together. She found humor in taking something to its odd limit. "I was never going to make you urinate on a fire hydrant. I got you a kitty litter box."

Her outraged gasp filled his soul with joy. "Eric!"

The traffic eased and he let off the brake. They had another ten or fifteen minutes until they got to the club. He could convince her. "Baby, that would fall under water sport and we agreed not to do that. Relax. It's nothing more than a little fun role-play."

"I'm not sure how pretending to be a puppy is going to be fun," she groused. "Getting to play with a bunch of puppies, now that would be fun."

"I'll try to arrange that for you." Maybe for her birthday. Certainly there had to be a place where he could rent puppies. Maybe. Her birthday was a couple of months away. He had some time. But he only had another couple of minutes to convince her to play his pet for the night. He'd been looking forward to it all week long. "But for tonight all you have to do is follow my lead and everything will be all right."

She frowned his way. "Will I have to crawl around?"

"I think you'll likely be a lap puppy." He wouldn't want her very far away. He'd gotten used to having her on his lap most of the time when they were in the club. "You might sit at my feet, but I promise I won't make you do anything you don't want to. Have I ever done that?"

"Well, I wasn't thrilled about the plug." She leaned against her side of the truck, her head resting pensively against the glass of the window. Her eyes stared out ahead, but he knew the expression. She got it when she was thinking too much, when she felt too much. "No, you haven't. It'll be fine. I'm sure I'll enjoy it."

Something was off with her. He'd noticed it when he'd picked her up. No plug for her tonight since she likely would end up in some odd positions. At first he'd wondered if she seemed off because he'd changed their routine. Now he wondered. "We don't have to play at all tonight if you don't want to."

She gave him a half smile. "I can handle puppy play, Eric. Most of the BDSM stuff is weird at first and then I enjoy it. It's opened me to a lot of new experiences." She was quiet for a moment. "I'm enjoying myself. I don't think I would be if you weren't my Dom."

And that scared her. He wasn't a fool. "Well, I am. You're doing very well. I think you'll breeze through the rest of the class."

She was suddenly interested in the view outside again. "I hope so. I've got a lot of changes coming up in my life. More than one graduation."

He was well aware that she was going to graduate from college soon. He'd been looking into presents for his smart, hard-working sub. "Are you excited about it? You've worked very hard. Not many people can get through college in four years while working a full-time job. You should be very proud of yourself."

She slid him a long look. "It was four and a half years, but who's counting? And I haven't graduated yet. It's going to be odd to not go to school every day. It's been a very long while since I had anything vaguely resembling free time."

"Have you thought about taking some time for yourself?" He wondered if she would take a trip or do something to celebrate.

She shook her head. "No." She was quiet for a moment. "There's something I haven't told you."

He took the exit and turned right, his gut knotting. He didn't like the tone of her voice, the sadness he heard behind it. "What is it?

Deena, you can tell me anything. I would rather know."

"I have a job lined up in Fort Worth."

He breathed a sigh of relief. He knew that. Did he think she could tell Tiffany and Ally something and not have it get all around the restaurant? "Of course you do. I didn't think you would stay working as a waitress after you finished college. It's kind of the point of finishing college. No one expected you to stay on at Top."

"Oh." Her shoulders dropped as though that wasn't the response she'd been expecting.

It was these moments that gave him hope. She didn't like the fact that he wasn't flipping out over the idea of her leaving. He had some news of his own. "I'm leaving Top, too."

"What?" She turned fully in her seat as he pulled up to the gate and put in his access code. "You can't leave Top. You're the sous chef. Oh my god, is this because you had that drink with Tim Love?"

It was not freaking disloyal to have a damn Scotch with another chef. "No. I'm opening a franchise of Top in Fort Worth. I already found a space right off Sundance Square. I'd really like for you to take a look at it with me this weekend."

He eased through the gated entrance. Before Eric had joined the club there had been some douchebag who had blown up the first building. Big Tag took no chances now. The entryway was closed with a super heavy gate that it would likely take a tank to get through, and Eric wouldn't be surprised if there were snipers watching him right now. From what he'd heard, the newbies at McKay-Taggart had their own crap jobs to do before being deemed fit for the field, and one of them was working security for Sanctum.

"Are you serious?" Deena got the goofiest grin on her face. "You're opening your own place?"

A little thrill went through him every time he thought about it. His place. It could be her place, too, though she wouldn't be waiting tables. "I'm basically going into business with the Taggarts, but it's going to be mine."

She was quiet for a moment, her hands in her lap as he pulled into his parking space. He got out of the car but she stayed inside. Another thing he'd trained her to do. He opened her door and helped her down since his truck was a bit oversized and he didn't want her to twist her ankle jumping out of it. That was a bit of a lie. He simply wanted that moment when she was in his arms, that second when she held on to him for support before finding her footing.

He opened the door and suddenly he was the one trying not to fall. She launched herself at him, her arms and legs winding around him.

"I'm so happy for you!" She let out a squeal and kissed him as she held on. "You're going to be Chef!"

He held on to her, loving the way she felt in his arms. "It's still a franchise and I have to run the big things by Sean. He and Big Tag are helping finance me. It's going to be a while before I'm all on my own."

"I'm so proud of you," she whispered in his ear. "You deserve it, Eric. You're an amazing chef and you're going to be an awesome boss." She kissed him again, this time on the cheek. "But you should hire a business manager because you suck at math."

He eased her down, not letting go even when she was steady. "I suck at math?"

She chuckled but wouldn't back down. "You do. Oh, you can do all the fractions you like, but I've seen you try to balance a checkbook and you get angry at it."

"The banks deliberately make that confusing." He defended himself even though he knew she was right.

She shook her head, her hands running up his side as though she couldn't help but touch him. "Nope. They do try to make it easy. It's all money in and money out. What's going to happen when you have to add in projection costs and…oh, no, the dreaded payroll accounting."

Thank god he could cook because all those other things kind of gave him the hives. "I was hoping that someone smarter than me would kind of guide me down that path. Maybe some super intelligent woman who managed to put herself through college and who's about to earn a highly rated business degree."

She stepped back and that wall between them seemed to slam into place again. "Wow, uhm, of course I'll look at your plans, but like I said, I have a job lined up."

What had put that look on her face? Did she think he was trying to use her? "Hey, I wasn't asking you to work for free. I would pay you a consultation fee."

She shook her head and seemed to brush it off. "Don't be silly. I would love to take a look at your business plan and very likely tear it apart and tell you all the places you're going wrong. No. Seriously, I'll give it a look and tell you what I think. And I would love to see the space. I like the Sundance location, but you better have foot traffic."

He was relieved the awkward moment had passed. "I absolutely have foot traffic. And the Bass is right down the street. I thought I could pick up some of the after-theater crowd."

She went up on her toes and gave him a quick kiss. "Good. E-mail it to me or print it out and bring in what you have and I'll give you my opinion. My new job happens to be in downtown Fort Worth, so I expect free lunches. Also, I'm not wearing a puppy collar. I'm a free-range puppy. I'm very well trained."

He would simply leave the pink collar and leash he'd bought for her in his locker and she would never have to know. "Of course."

She grinned then turned and started to walk toward the club. Damn, but he liked to watch her walk, her hips swaying.

He should have thought about that leash. She'd been leashed for much of her life. It would rankle. She enjoyed submission on a sexual level. It gave her permission to enjoy the sex, but Deena would always need to know she was a partner in play. It was why he feared she wouldn't enjoy life with some random Dom who wouldn't understand why she was here and what she needed deep down.

He followed her, feeling more optimistic than he had before.

* * * *

Eric was leaving Top. Eric was starting his own restaurant. Eric wasn't Eddie.

That was her new mantra. She looked down at the pretty sapphire-colored corset and tiny PVC mini she was wearing, sure reminders of the fact that her new friend wasn't anything like her old husband. Eddie had rarely bought her a birthday gift, much less something as decadent and luxurious as a new set of fet wear. It had been waiting for her the day after what she now referred to as Butt Plug Armageddon. Once Eric had decided to take control, he'd bought her three new sets of club wear. There was the one she was wearing, a super slutty mini dress with fuck me heels, and a red corset with the tiniest thong she'd ever seen. They all made her feel sexy and just the right side of trashy and…

Taken care of. Those stupid clothes made her feel taken care of.

Though he'd merely said he enjoyed buying clothes for his sub and hinted that he would do it for any sub, she wasn't stupid. He'd done it for her because he'd seen the sad state of her clothes and understood how they made her feel.

He was too good to be true. Had she found the flaw? He needed business help and she was good at business. Everyone knew what her degree was in. Well, if she managed to pass.

"You look very serious for a girl about to bark all night," Tiff said with a glint in her eye.

She stared at her friend through the mirror. It was all happening so fast. It was going to be hard to leave Top, but she would still have this club.

Maybe.

How would she handle seeing Eric with another sub? Their contract only lasted so long and she already knew how dangerous it would be to sign another with him. If she let herself, she would fall in love with the man, and that couldn't happen.

She forced the thoughts away and closed her locker, turning to Tiffany. "I am not a yippy puppy. I'm a free-range puppy. You let him put a collar on you?"

Tiffany was wearing a thin silver collar around her neck that was attached to a rhinestone-studded leash. She laughed and waved off the thought. "It's only play, D. It's not like I'm actually a puppy. Gage and I are having some fun. I'm pretty sure that when I start chewing on his leathers I can get him to swat my ass with a rolled up newspaper."

Sounded like a fun Thursday night. "I don't know. It kind of freaks me out a little."

Tiff sighed and leaned against the lockers. "Because you already had one man treat you like shit and you had to watch your mom go through it, too. I, on the other hand, was treated like a princess by Mommy and Daddy and therefore can have a sense of humor about the whole dog thing. Also, growing up my mother always had a Maltese. Seriously, they were all named Gucci and we numbered them. When my mom died, she was buried in a coffin that smelled like Chanel and we had to get special permission to inter the dogs' ashes with her. The mausoleum my parents want me to one day join them in also houses six Maltese dogs in designer urns. Somewhere in heaven they're yipping and eating caviar while my mom lunches with Audrey Hepburn."

Tiffany had an odd life. A sudden thought hit Deena. Tiff adored her father and he came into Top on a regular basis, but she never talked much about her upbringing. Deena only knew it had been privileged. "Tell me you weren't named for the jewelry store."

Tiff winced. "Sorry, can't do it. Have you met my sisters, Burberry and Versace? I got the easy end of that stick."

"Why are you doing this training class and the internship? You could afford to buy a membership to Sanctum."

"Number one, I like babies so the idea of paying my way into a membership by watching babies doesn't bother me at all. I would do that for free. Babies make me happy. My sisters will never have them. Berry says having children would ruin her figure and she's trying to become a supermodel. I tried to tell her that years of eating like crap already ruined her figure, but she's an optimist, and V is living in a tent in France because she doesn't want to leave a footprint on the fragile earth. Her words, not mine. She'll probably have a ton of kids because she thinks birth control pills will give her cancer, so she counts the days on some weird beaded stick thing. Yeah, those beads aren't going to stop Frenchie's sperm, but she thinks she knows better. Number two, I don't have a lot of money. My dad does. Would he give it to me? In a heartbeat. The trouble is he raised me way too well. He raised me to want to make something of myself. What can I say? I want to make my dad proud and that means working hard. Number three, I want to paint."

"You can paint without starving."

"Yes, but what would I paint? What would it mean? The world is a way bigger place than it seems. I want to see it, be a part of it, and I can't do that if I'm behind some ornate wall designed by Karl Lagerfeld. At the end of the day everyone has it rough. That's what I've figured out. Rich, poor, beautiful, or unattractive we all have something to get through and it always feels like the end of the world. It's what makes us human."

She had a point, but still. "Some people have it worse than others."

"There is always someone who has it worse than you. Always someone who has it better. If you spend your whole life comparing good and bad, you're going to come up short, D. And you're going to waste what time you have. My mom had it great. She had money and love and everything a person could ask for, and she also got terminal cancer at the age of forty-six. That was her life, the good and the bad. And when she went, it was in style because my mother knew how to live. While she fought I never once heard her complain or bemoan her fate."

"Because she knew she had it so good."

"No, because she wouldn't waste the time she had on fear and regret." Tiff reached out and smoothed back Deena's hair. "So I'm going to go and be a puppy and bark and yip like old Gucci and see if I can have some fun."

She made it sound so easy. Deena knew she wasn't talking about the puppy play. Tiffany was talking about Eric. Everyone seemed to talk about Eric around her these days, like they were already some established couple and she needed to run everything by him before making a decision.

She didn't need a damn man to make a decision for her.

But wouldn't it be better to have a real partner? Not someone who made decisions for her, but someone who helped her, who stood by her even when she made the wrong move.

"Hey, did you talk to Chef about your test?" Tiffany started to walk toward the door. They were the last two left in the locker room. If they didn't get their butts in gear, there would be some puppy punishment in their future.

She shook her head. "It's not his problem. It's my shift. You're already working and Ally and Macon have plans that night with his family."

"What about Jenni?"

"I already asked Jenni. She's got a concert she's going to. Sure it doesn't start until after the restaurant closes, but how is she going to do her hair if she has to work?"

"Selfish bitch. I totally worked a shift for her so she could go on a date. I'll talk to her. Or punch her in the face. One of the two."

She did not want to cause a fight. "I'll make due."

Tiffany stopped her. "If you don't pass this test, you don't graduate."

Didn't she know it. Her last class was being watched over by an asshole professor who seemed to enjoy making life tough for undergrads. Their entire grade was the final. No graded homework. No participation. No way to even know if they were getting the material. One test would decide if she graduated on time or had to refuse her dream job because she would no longer be qualified. Everything was riding on that stupid test and she couldn't get anyone to cover her shift.

She could call in sick, but that would put the burden on everyone else. Or she could suck it up and study after shift when her brain no longer functioned.

"If you won't talk to Chef, tell Eric." Tiffany opened the door. "He can make things happen."

That seemed too intimate. They played together. They didn't do serious things like figuring out problems. She needed to keep it light and casual so when the time came she could walk away.

God, she already didn't want to walk away. She was in too deep. She was bargaining and their contract wasn't up yet. Maybe they could keep up the D/s relationship. At the time she'd thought he would live in Dallas and she would only see him on club nights. That would be cool.

But now he was going to be living near her. He would want more. He would end up wanting everything she had.

"I'll think about it," she murmured.

"Don't think about it too long," Tiffany replied as she waved to Gage. "It's coming up fast. Hey, maybe we could put Bas in a server uniform and make him wait tables. I would pay to see that show."

"Bas?" Surely she wasn't talking about the very proper Sebastian.

Tiffany shrugged. "He needed a nickname to work against that two by four someone shoved up his muscular backside."

She could see Eric on the other side of the dungeon. He was already set up with a chair. One for both of them. Maybe tonight wouldn't be so different. She sat in his lap every night. It was kind of nice. Wait. What had she said? "How do you know Sebastian has a muscular backside?"

"Is that the way puppies move?" Gage called out across the room.

Tiffany wrinkled her nose and dropped to her knees. "I swear I would chew his shoe all up but he wears them in the ER, so I could get some horrible disease. And I know about Sebastian's backside because it was pretty much on display at my house the night you sent me home with the bastard. He wears tighty-whities by the way. Super muscular buns. He must do a ton of squats. Are you going to make me do this alone? I'll stop talking and bark all the way across the dungeon."

Deena groaned, facing a tough decision. Dignity or gossip. Damn it. She dropped down. The floors at Sanctum were kept very clean and there were anti-bac stations all over the place. She would survive. She started crawling, matching Tiffany's pace. "You slept with the sommelier?"

"No, but he apparently thought I was too drunk to be left alone, so he was asleep on my couch and he'd pushed off the blanket and I got a look at that butt. Gorgeous butt. Too bad it's attached to him. Pretentious ass." Tiffany sighed. "He got all huffy because I saw him without his legs on."

"Legs? I thought he only lost one."

"Nope, it's both, and what he has left is all hot, too, but the man himself is twelve kinds of prissy. I got a big old lecture on how I shouldn't drink to excess because it will ruin my palate and how it's impolite to stare at a man's legs. Or rather his non-legs. I tried to explain that I was looking at his ass, but that only pissed him off more. Did you know he's already got Master's rights here?"

"Wow, how did he get them but not Eric?" She scooted along, praying her boobs didn't fall out.

"Rumor has it, he spent a lot of time at some club in London and the owner vouched for him. It's Sanctum's sister club. I am not looking forward to being in the same dungeon with that man. Well, I am, but I'm not because he makes me feel all crappy about stuff I shouldn't have to feel crappy about. I told him he could look at my butt if it would make him feel better and he said something very uptight and left."

"Look at that," a deep voice said. "Our puppies are playing and not doing what they were commanded to do. Sit up, Tiffany."

Her friend immediately sat up, her hands coming in front of her chest like little paws, and she made a yipping sound, but not before she'd winked Deena's way.

Gage stood in front of her, picking up her leash in one hand while he tapped a crop against his leg with the other. "Bad puppy. Bad puppies get spanked."

Gage brought the crop down on Tiffany's ass and she yelped, playing her part to the hilt. She and Gage started to play. Eric simply leaned over and picked her up. She was lifted into his strong arms.

"My puppy is a lap dog. She doesn't like to get her paws dirty." Eric smiled down at her as he started to walk back toward the stage. "I was surprised to see you crawling. Have you changed your mind?"

Why were his big arms so comfy? He was the only man who'd ever carried her around and she liked it more than she cared to admit. "I had to crawl next to Tiffany to find out how she'd seen the sommelier in his undies."

Eric's eyes went wide and he stopped briefly. "She slept with Sebastian? I knew she wasn't sleeping with Gage, but I'm shocked she's into Sebastian. They seem so different."

He seemed to know some gossip she didn't. Tiffany hadn't said much about her training Dom beyond the fact that she enjoyed playing with him. They actually made a very hot couple. "How do you know she's not sleeping with him? Everyone else seems to be sleeping together. I'm pretty sure Althea's doing her sub."

"Oh, yeah, those two are fucking like rabbits. Well, one very submissive Harvard-educated rabbit and Althea. But Gage is married. His wife's a top, too. She's already got Mistress rights and Gage wanted to give it a try. They intend to play and top subs but without sex. It'll be interesting to see how that works out," Eric explained. "But I want to hear that story about Tiff and Sebastian after the class.

For now, be my sweet puppy. We're going to watch a scene and then play for a bit."

He settled into his seat, never once showing a single sign that she weighed a thing.

Ian Taggart stepped onto the stage in front of them. "Welcome bitches."

"Ian!" Charlotte wasn't far behind him.

Big Tag shrugged. "It's puppy play night, baby. I apologize. I'm supposed to be more correct in my speech. Welcome owners, bitches, and dog." He nodded toward the lone male sub in the room. "Sorry, Keen. Male puppies are just dogs and you should be very good tonight because I've heard Althea's into cock and ball torture, so you might find yourself neutered."

"I believe I asked you to be more politically correct in your speech," Charlotte muttered.

"Yeah, that's not going to happen, baby." Master Ian held up a long cylindrical object. "Get your puppies settled and let's talk about violet wands. This particular one is about to light up my mouthy puppy's nipples."

Eric's hands began to move over her thighs and down to her knees before coming back up. "My puppy needs to be petted. She's very anxious today. Like a shaky Chihuahua. Here, pretty girl, have a treat." He pulled a chocolate out of a baggy he'd set beside them. "Macon made them specially for sweet puppies."

Macon's handmade chocolates. When she reached for it, Eric pulled his hand away. Of course. Puppies ate from their Master's hands. Well, except Harrison apparently. Althea had a dog bowl set up for him. Yeah, Deena was happy her Master knew what she could and couldn't take. She leaned forward and wrapped her lips around his fingers, taking the chocolate from his hand and giving him a lick as she pulled back and enjoyed the rich taste.

Eric's hands moved over her, petting her constantly. She settled in and relaxed. Being his pet wasn't so bad.

Three hours later, she kind of wished she had the courage to ask Eric to come inside and spend the night with her. He pulled into her parking lot and put the car into park. He always did this. He would walk her upstairs and make sure she locked the door. At first she'd been able to hear her mother in her head complaining that the man obviously didn't think she had any sense if he didn't believe she could lock her door on her own. Her mother had taken a dim view of the men in her life playing at being gentlemen. "Playing" being the operative word.

Deena, if some boy is opening doors for you and carrying your books to class, it's because he's trying to get into your pants. Once you give it up, you'll see the real man and trust me, honey, it won't be pretty.

Of course she'd already given it up for Eric and he still insisted on this ritual every night. The door closed on his side and she waited.

Had she picked Eddie because he hadn't done any of those things for her? Because he'd claimed she was an equal and wouldn't insult her by opening a door she could open herself? Had she trusted that more than she did a man who treated her well?

"Deena?"

She hadn't even noticed when he'd opened the door. Her gut was knotted because of what was happening next week. Her final. She had to work the four nights before her final in statistics, and naturally that wasn't the only final she had to worry about. How was she going to feel if she failed? She could try again next semester. Calling the company she was supposed to start working for would be the worst part. Having to explain that she'd failed...

"I wish you would tell me what's wrong," he said quietly. "I know you don't believe it, but I want to help."

That was the problem. She was starting to believe he did. She was beginning to depend on him, and everything she'd been taught led her to believe that was wrong. It wasn't a good idea to depend on anyone but herself. It was fine to have friends, fine to help them, but she was different. She was independent.

"It's nothing. I'm tired. I should get some sleep." Turning to get out of the truck, she found herself blocked by his big body.

His hands went to her waist, his face close to hers. "Tell me and let me help. Was it the puppy play? Did it make you feel small? Feeling small doesn't have to mean something bad. You can be small in my arms and still be taken care of."

This was the last thing she wanted. She leaned back and put her hands on either side of his face, looking into his eyes so he would understand. "I liked it. It was fun, Eric. I liked being stroked and pampered. That's not what's bothering me."

"Then tell me what is."

She'd been a puppy but now he was a dog with a bone. "I have a final next week and I'm worried about it and I have to work all week long because no one can swap shifts with me."

He sighed and stepped back, holding out a hand. "Is that all? I thought it was serious. Come on. Let's get you upstairs. I have to do the farmer's market run in the morning because Sean is taking Carys for a checkup."

She took his hand, oddly disappointed that he wasn't making a bigger deal out of this. She'd kind of expected him to offer to fix the problem, but he seemed more concerned with getting home to bed. That was good. Wasn't it? He recognized that she could handle herself. It was good.

It wasn't Eric. It was kind of shitty.

She followed him upstairs, her key in hand. She would start studying now. She would do it on breaks and during her very nonexistent off time, and she would maybe skip a training class next week. Surely Master Ian would understand. It would all work out if she tried hard enough.

Eric watched her walk inside. "How many days do you need?"

She could start studying tonight. Who needed sleep? "For what?"

He chuckled. "For studying, silly girl. How quickly your brain moves on to other things. How many nights do you need off so you can feel ready for your test?"

"Oh, I was only looking for one. I was trying to take next Thursday off since I take the test on Friday."

He nodded and leaned over, brushing a kiss across her lips. "You're off Wednesday and Thursday. Don't worry about a thing. I'll handle it. You study and pass because I kind of need a smart girl to help me out. One of us needs to finish college. Lock the door, baby. I'll see you tomorrow."

"Eric, I..."

"Goodnight." He pulled the door closed. "Lock it."

She twisted the deadbolt and put her hand against the door, standing there until she heard his truck take off.

What the hell was she going to do with that man?

CHAPTER EIGHT

Eric forced his legs to work. Two straight days of being on his feet for twelve hours a day had damn near ruined him, but he wanted to check in with Deena. The last week had been rough. She'd been studying like crazy and getting ready for the end of the term. He'd backed off after offering to help and being gently rebuffed. She claimed she wasn't able to concentrate while he was around. He wasn't sure if that was a point in his favor or one more obstacle between them.

There seemed to be so damn many of those.

She'd accepted his help but then he'd felt the distance between them again. Deena hadn't turned cold exactly. She was still accepting his rides to and from work, still sitting in his lap, and still getting hot for him when he turned on the D/s sex. Unfortunately, she managed to turn all sex into D/s sex. If he tried to kiss her, she pushed him until he dominated her.

He had to face facts. A D/s relationship might be all she wanted from him. Was he willing to accept that? Was he willing to sign another contract with her?

He stopped on the landing and sighed. Yeah, he probably was. He was willing to do almost anything to stay with her. What did that make him? He wasn't sure it was making him happy.

He glanced down at his watch. It was past midnight. He should be back at Top eating with the crew, having a glass of whatever Sebastian had paired with the duck they'd served tonight, but no, he was here stalking a woman who didn't truly want him.

He was about to turn and walk back to the parking lot when her door flew open.

"Eric?"

He put on his best face. Caught red-handed. That was him. "Hey, I was coming to make sure you had everything you needed."

She put a hand over her chest and took a long breath. "I heard your truck, but then you didn't knock. I was worried something had happened. Come in. It's not the best neighborhood."

Eric found himself being led into her tiny apartment. He'd had some fairly dirty sex in that apartment, but he hadn't slept over and she'd found a reason to refuse overnight invites to his place. He stepped inside as she closed and locked the door behind them. To his left was her small dining room table. It was covered with books and papers. It looked like Deena was burning the midnight oil. "Which is why you should think about moving."

It was a sketchy part of town, but it was likely all she could afford, and he doubted offering to let her move in with him would work at this point.

She walked into the kitchen. "I'm going to do that once I graduate. How about you? Are you going to make the commute into Fort Worth or are you moving?"

It was the most interest she'd shown in him in days. "I'm looking for a place close to the restaurant, but we've got a couple of months before we're ready to open. The lawyers are coming in next week to finalize the deal."

Her eyes had flared and for a moment he'd thought she was going to ask him questions about the restaurant, but she turned her attention to the teakettle on the stove instead. "I would have thought you would be eating at Top right now. Did we close early?"

He hadn't wanted to chance missing her. He'd figured she would still be awake at this point, but she did have a test in the morning. "Everything ran all right, but I'd been there all day and I wanted to head home. I thought I'd check on you. I can see everything is going okay so I'll get out of your hair."

She stepped out of the kitchen. "You worked my shifts, didn't you?"

He'd hoped she wouldn't figure that out. "I can take an order and handle front of house."

"After you prepped the full menu and in between checking up on everyone," she surmised.

He shrugged. It was what needed to be done. "It's fine. You'll be back Saturday night and everything will continue on. Well, until you turn in your notice."

"Sit down, please, Sir. Let me get you a beer."

How nice would that be? Unfortunately, he had to drive and as tired as he was, he didn't want to chance falling asleep at the wheel. "I should go."

A single brow rose above one blue eye. "Or you could stay here and let me take care of you for once."

"Deena, I'll fall asleep on your couch."

She moved in, stepping close to him and smoothing down his shirt with the palms of her hands. "Then go lay down in the bed."

Was she serious? "I'll fall asleep. I've been up and on my feet for hours."

"Because you were doing your job and mine." Her arms wrapped around him, her head finding his chest. "You didn't have to do that."

"I did."

"Why?"

"Because I care about you."

Her arms squeezed him. "That scares me, but I care about you, too. I missed seeing you the past two days. I missed you more than I thought I would. I've gotten used to being around you."

He let himself relax a fraction, sliding his arms around her body. Damn, but that felt good. "I missed you, too."

It had been a ridiculously long week. He'd backed off and given her space. He didn't want to make her choose between him and her schoolwork. He would lose that battle and he should. He simply couldn't find a way to make her understand that he didn't want her to choose. He wanted to help her attain her goals. So he'd tried to show her instead.

"I'm going to be so glad to kiss this professor good-bye," she said with one last squeeze. "Can I make you a sandwich?"

He was staying. It was weird. He found himself watching her, trying to figure out what had happened. "Do you have anything to make a sandwich with?"

She was wearing a pair of pajama bottoms and a tank top that didn't hide the fact that her nipples were hard as little jewels. "Of course. I have some cheap ham. At least the package says it's ham."

"How about I take us out for breakfast in the morning instead. I'm beat. I don't want to disrupt your studying." He couldn't help his yawn. It had been a long day. "You sure you don't want me to go home?"

She stared at him for a moment, her mind obviously spinning. "I think you going home would be easy for me, but it's not what I want. I've thought a lot the last couple of days. Really ever since the puppy play night. I've thought about what's going to happen when we graduate from the training program."

They were going to do this here and now? He wasn't sure he was ready for that. "What do you think is going to happen?"

"I've gone through two scenarios," she said thoughtfully. "One is that you shake my hand and wish me well and we see each other and play from time to time. We're kind of friends. Maybe even good friends, but we have our own lives and only see each other at the club."

Was she high? "I don't know that's the most likely scenario. I think the more likely scenario is you walk away and we don't really talk and we're not truly friends."

"And then I would have to watch you with other subs and that would bug me, Eric." She bit her bottom lip and her eyes slid away. "So I have to move on to scenario number two."

He was still, like "don't try to scare the deer who might finally try to eat out of his hand" still. "What's that, baby?"

"You offer me a collar."

"I already bought one," he said quietly. If she was going to be honest with him, he wasn't going to hide the truth. He'd bought it days ago. "Though it's not actually a collar. It's more like a necklace. Like what Sean gave Grace."

Her face had flushed and she nodded. "Yes, I probably wouldn't like a real collar for the daytime." Her eyes closed and then opened again. "I don't know what to say. I hadn't thought that far yet. I only know that I reject scenario number one. Can I have some time to think about the collar?"

She was bending. It was all he could ask. Relief flooded through him. They still had so much to work out, but he had hope. "Of course. How about you promise me this—when we graduate we'll continue playing together like we have. I won't play with anyone except you. We'll find a couple of apartments in Fort Worth and we'll see where this goes."

Her smile made his heart pound. "Yes. That would be great."

He took two steps and was in front of her, leaning over and brushing a kiss on her lips. "For now, don't worry about anything other than tomorrow's test. I'll take care of the rest. As for the future, we'll take it one day at a time."

She went up on her toes and kissed him again. "Thank you, Eric."

"But I would appreciate it if you would look at my business plan once you're done with school," he insisted. He wanted her feedback. He didn't want to screw this thing up. "And I would love it if you would come with me when I sign the paperwork. Lawyers give me the hives and I haven't even met this one. Mitchell Bradford won't work both sides. Apparently he developed morals or something. It's all agreed on, but I'm still nervous. At the end of the day, I'm just an old SEAL who learned how to cook. I don't understand the rest of it."

She pulled away. "Eric, I don't know about that. I think it might be best if we kept that part of our lives separate."

"What do you mean?"

"I mean the work part. When I said we could see each other, I was talking about in the club. You can pick me up and we can have dinner or something, but I don't know that I want to be involved in your business."

That was about as plainly as she could put it. He knew why she was saying it, but it still felt like a kick in the nuts. "We're going to be living in a new city and working demanding jobs. You don't want to even talk about our work? I'm going to be starting up a business, Deena. It's going to take most of my time. I suppose when I said we would see each other, I kind of saw you coming in and having dinner and hanging out."

"Hanging out? Or doing your books and making sure you get free business advice?"

He put a hand up. "I wasn't thinking of it that way. I don't know, maybe I was. Not the free part. Of course, I can pay you for the initial consult. I guess when I really think about starting up, I saw you with me. When I think of building this restaurant, I see us working together."

"That's not going to happen. I have a job, Eric. It's a good job."

He knew that. He knew it was a long shot. "Like I said, if you'll take a look at the plan, I'll pay you. I won't ask you to do anything beyond that. If you only want to see me at the club, then that's how it will be. I think I am going to head home."

She caught him before he reached the door. "Please stay. I'm sorry. I was harsh and we're both tired. Can we talk about this in the morning?"

Would anything change? Did any of it matter if this kept coming between them? "I'm trying not to push you, Deena, but knowing that you think I would use you that way doesn't bode well for the two of us. Maybe you're right and we should keep everything separate."

"Or we can sleep on it and talk about it again tomorrow," she said quietly. "When you're supposed to take me to breakfast so I don't have to eat stale cereal again. Please, Eric. I'm sorry. I meant what I said the first time. I need a little time, but I know now that I don't need to spend that time away from you."

"Even the time you spend with me…is all you want D/s?" He knew he was pushing her and he'd said he wouldn't, but he needed to know the answer to that particular question. He could be patient, but if all she ever wanted was a relationship that occurred in a club and with quick couplings, he would have to rethink. The idea that she didn't really want him shook him to his core.

"I don't know." There were tears in her eyes and that was what forced his hand.

He leaned over with a long sigh and kissed her forehead. "All right. We'll talk more in the morning. What side of the bed do you want?"

He couldn't leave her crying. Not even to save his own pride. And who knew? Maybe things would look better in the morning. Or maybe they would be very clear and it would be easier to have a frank discussion about breaking it all off. The one thing he knew? They weren't fixing shit tonight.

"I tend to sleep on the right. I think I might snore."

He chuckled because she made it sound like the worst thing a person could do. "I can handle it."

"Actually, I've been told I sound like a dying water buffalo."

Was that why she wouldn't sleep with him? God, if he ever met her ex-husband he would pound the man into the ground. All of their problems seemed to stem from that asswipe. "Somehow, I'll make it through. Good night."

He turned and walked down the short hall that led to the only bedroom. Deena's bedroom was oddly utilitarian, as though she'd gone through a discount housewares store and bought whatever was on sale and not a bit more than was required. There was a dresser and a double bed that his legs would likely hang off. Her bedspread was a plain dark blue matching the pillows. Those pillows weren't decorative though. He'd had a girlfriend whose whole bed was covered in pretty pillows that she had to move every time she got into bed. She'd claimed they made her happy.

There was nothing in Deena's bedroom that looked like it made her happy. He was beginning to wonder if he could make her happy.

What was he doing? He knew when to walk away. He'd done it before when it was obvious a relationship simply wasn't going to work. Why couldn't he do it now?

Because he wanted her more than he'd ever wanted another woman. Because he knew deep down if he could get past those walls she'd built around herself that she was the one. She was the one for him. He was the one for her. They could make a life together if only she wanted to.

He kicked off his boots and tried to let it go. He shrugged out of his shirt and got down to his boxers. Every muscle in his body ached and earlier he'd been cool with that. Earlier it had been proof that he was helping out the woman he was crazy about. Now it was just pain.

He turned off the light and pulled down the bedspread. He lay down, but didn't cover up because it was hot in her bedroom. He would cool off in a few minutes. His eyes drifted closed, but he couldn't shut his brain down.

"Turn over."

He opened his eyes and she was standing beside him. She'd spoken to him quietly, but there had been some command in her voice. It rankled since all she seemed to require from him was dominance. "Excuse me?"

She must have heard the chill in his tone because she softened. "I'm sorry. Eric, would you please turn over and let me rub your back?"

"You don't have to do that."

"I want to. Please."

He rolled over, wondering what she was thinking. She'd never offered him service before. Not anything he hadn't asked for or the training course hadn't required. He felt her straddle him, her backside against his, and then something cool hit his skin.

"It's a little baby oil," she said and he could hear the grin in her voice. "It's not lube or anything, though I now have like a gallon supply of that stashed in here. I worry that my mom will show up and decide the place needs a thorough cleaning. She'll find a whole bunch of stuff you've left here."

Sex toys and rope. It wasn't like he'd left clothes here or a toothbrush. Just sex toys. "I can put them in the truck if they bother you."

She was quiet for a moment and then her hands smoothed over his back. Fuck, that felt good.

"I was joking. I don't mind if my mom finds out I'm a pervert." She ran her thumbs along his spine, causing him to groan with pleasure. "I don't talk about my marriage very often, but maybe we should discuss it now. You need to understand why I can't throw myself into a relationship very easily. It's a long story."

Her sheets smelled like lavender. He breathed in the scent and let himself relax. "Because your first husband managed to convince you to pay his way through law school and then ditched you the first chance he got, and now you think all men are out to use you and throw you away."

"Okay, when you put it like that it's not such a long story." She went to work on his shoulders. "My dad ditched me, too. It was me and my mom."

"She didn't date?"

"God, no. She was done with men. She told me she wouldn't ever put me through that again. She was really angry when I got married so young. I can still remember that lecture. Hadn't I learned anything? Why was I supporting a husband and not getting my own education? I think she mostly called me a fool those first couple of years. I thought I was building a life with him."

"You also likely thought you could prove your mother wrong." He'd seen that before. Hell, he'd been young and dumb. Kids almost always found some way to rebel even when they were raised well. It was natural.

"I suppose. It was hard to have to tell her I failed."

Though the massage felt amazing, he couldn't let that pass. With ease he flipped her over, maneuvering his body to pin hers down. Suddenly he wasn't all that tired. He was well aware that they were in a bed together for the first time. He let her feel his weight. "You did not fail."

If she was bothered by him taking control, she damn sure didn't show it. Her hands came up, caressing his torso. "It felt like I did. I don't ever want to feel like that again. It's why I'm worried about what's happening between us. I thought I could keep it casual, but it's not."

At least she was finally admitting it. "No, it's not casual. Definitely not for me. I am not your ex-husband."

"I know that intellectually, but it's hard to understand it emotionally. I know I'm tough to deal with. I'm not your dream sub, but I'm going to try harder. Stay the night with me. I'm tired of sleeping alone. I never minded it before. I liked it for a long time, but now I simply lay in bed and think about you."

He couldn't help the way his whole body seemed to shrug off the aches in favor of one righteous erection. "Baby, I think we're going to need a bigger bed."

* * * *

She loved the way he pinned her down. Why had she been so afraid of this? Somehow she always managed to have sex with Eric in a position that wasn't very intimate. She would maneuver her body until she was facing away from him or riding him and leaning back.

He pressed her into the bed as his mouth found hers and she was surrounded by his heat. So warm. She was always cold, but when Eric was around she could snuggle against him and get warm wherever they happened to be.

He was so big and somehow so gentle with her. Even when he was rough, she wasn't afraid of him. He would never hurt her physically. No, that wasn't her issue. Looking into his eyes seemed too intimate, too much. She'd always worried that if she looked into his eyes when he was deep inside her she would fall for him.

It was stupid because she'd pretty much already done that anyway.

His tongue plunged deep, sliding against hers, and she could feel him all around her. She wrapped herself up in him, tangling their limbs until it didn't feel like there was an inch of her skin that wasn't touched by some part of him. This was why she'd held out. This wasn't a quick fuck. It was a meshing of bodies, a long slow dance that she couldn't hold herself apart from. There was no way to take the pleasure from this experience without also accepting the intimacy. She could have sworn she could feel his heart beating against hers.

"This time you don't top from the bottom," he growled against her lips.

She shook her head, letting her hands play against the strong muscles of his shoulders and arms. "I don't do that."

He nipped at her ear, sending a thrill through her system. "You do it constantly, but it only annoys me during sex. That's going to change. I'm more than willing to be the indulgent Dom in the vanilla world, but this is our private world and I'm in charge here."

She tried to figure out what he was talking about. "I let you tie me up and do what you want with me."

He pressed his torso up, looking her in the eyes. "No. You manipulate me until you get what you want. This is what I want. I want to be on top of you, inside you, with you wrapped up around me like you can't get enough. I want you with me. I don't want us to be two people getting off. I want more."

It scared her to death, but she did, too. "How can I please you,

Sir?"

His hips moved, rubbing that glorious cock of his up against her pajama bottoms. He'd stolen all her undies so it was only the thin cotton of her pants and his boxers that kept them apart. She would have protested the fact that he was allowed to wear undies and she wasn't, but that particular argument had almost led to losing bra privileges, and she wasn't risking that again. Sometimes her Dom was an immovable object.

And that was a good thing.

"I want to put my mouth on you."

She felt herself stiffen. She was pretty sure he wasn't talking about kissing her lips again. This was something she'd been trying to avoid. When he would start to roam down there, she would rub and twist and force them into a position that made oral impossible. Damn it, she did top from the bottom.

His hand found her hair and twisted lightly, forcing her gaze back to him. "Did he tell you you don't taste good?"

She hated the fact that her ex-husband was still here, still causing her issues. "Yes. He tried it once when we were first married and said he couldn't stand it. He never tried it again."

"Deena, I want you to listen to me and listen to me good. I am not that man. I will never be that man and I want that man out of our relationship. This is between you and me, and he has no place here so I will make my own decisions. I will say one more thing about him and then you're going to let that shit go for the rest of the night. He was a selfish little prick and he denied himself and you. You're better off without him and I'm going to show you why. You are not to think about what he said to you when I'm eating your pussy like it's the best piece of pie ever baked. Do you understand? That's going to be my mouth on you, my lips and tongue making you come, and make no mistake, you will come for me. You're going to love it when your Master tells you to spread your legs and let him have a taste of his pussy. Yeah, that pussy is mine and I'll lick and suck on it whenever I want from now on. Am I understood?"

When he talked like that, so dark, his tone deep and demanding, she couldn't help but respond. There was something in the core of her being that reacted to the way he took control. "Yes, Sir."

She couldn't fight him when he talked like that, couldn't even argue her point. Not about something like this. He wanted to kiss her there. He wouldn't be put off or listen to the reasons why it might not be a good idea. His will held sway here.

"You're to be still. Do you understand? I want you to reach up and grab the rods of the headboard and don't let go." He stared down at her. "This is the time when you can choose to disobey me and send this all into the spiral that leads to us fucking the way we have every time before. I'm asking you not to. I'm asking you to let us be what we can be."

He didn't seem to require her response, merely set forth his request. She could force his hand or finally give the man what he wanted. She'd fought him and for what? Because Eddie had been an ass? Because she was still worried about what he'd wanted or disliked?

Shouldn't she ask herself what she wanted? Did she want to feel Eric's tongue on her pussy? Yes. Yes, she pretty much couldn't think of anything she wanted more. She'd never had it before. Nothing beyond a single, pathetic lick that showed her nothing and then humiliation. Did she want to know what Serena's books talked about? Hell, yes.

She had to hope it wouldn't end the same way.

She let her hands drift up, finding the headboard and gripping it as he'd asked. She felt him shudder as though her submission had sent a wave of pleasure through him. He brushed his lips against hers before moving down her body. His lips moved over her neck. He licked at her, the sensation running through her. His hands moved to the top of her tank.

"I'll buy you a new one," he said right before he ripped it in two and bared her breasts. Her nipples were already hard nubs, begging for his attention. She couldn't care less about the tank top. She hated any fabric that came between them. She wanted to feel his skin against hers, the heat warming them both.

He kissed his way down her neck to her chest, his tongue coming out to lick at her nipple while his left hand tortured the other. His thumb rasped over the tip of her breast as he sucked the opposite one. She could feel his tongue whirling around and around, making her

139

womb clench. Shudders went through her system as wave after wave of arousal hit her.

Blood pounded through her body as he inched his way down. He kissed her stomach and dipped his tongue into her belly button before moving lower. His fingers dipped under the waistband of her PJ pants.

"Lift up."

She pushed her butt up, following his order. She found herself without pants very quickly. He got to his feet at the end of her bed and pulled them off her body. He was too big for her double. When she got her first paycheck from her new job, she would have to look into buying a new bed. A queen or maybe a king. Her Dom was a big guy. He needed his space, though she kind of thought he would end up being a cuddler.

"Spread your legs."

She moved them apart, already feeling herself getting warm and wet and ready. He was going to put his mouth on her. He was going to taste her, and that meant something to him. His hands wrapped around her ankles and pushed them up and further apart. She was utterly open to him, her female parts on full display.

She should be horrified, but somehow she knew Eric would like it. He would love her being spread and open and willing to do what he wanted. This was submission. She sank into it, allowing herself to slip out of her ordinary self-consciousness. There wasn't a place for it here. There was only what her Master wanted, what he needed from her. He spread her wide, splitting her open, and she couldn't help but take a deep breath and let it happen.

He settled himself on the bed. She couldn't see past his shoulders, but she would bet his knees were on the floor, his face right in her center. He looked up her body, his eyes locking with hers.

"I'm not thinking about anything but you." She needed him to know that he was all she thought about these days. Yes, her ex-husband and his cruelty sank in from time to time, but it was Eric who had her attention. She was insecure, but every time they played she gained confidence. Every time he touched her, she got closer to him, and unless she was willing to walk away, it wasn't going to change. She wasn't going to be able to protect herself from him.

"I'm going to make sure of it," he promised before lowering his head down.

A shudder went through her as she felt the heat of his breath along her feminine flesh. She tightened her grip on the headboard. Being still was already hard, but she was determined to give him this. She could see how selfish she'd been and she wanted to make him happy.

The first long drag of his tongue over her pussy made all those thoughts flee. This wasn't something to suffer through for his benefit. This was amazing.

"Stop squirming or I'll have to spank you," he warned, the words rumbling along her skin.

She went completely still because she did not want him to stop. Spanking was fun, but what he'd done was beyond amazing. A gasp puffed from her mouth as he licked her again.

"This is sheer perfection. Don't ever let anyone tell you this pussy isn't the best treat in the world. I should know," he said between nibbling bites. "This is sweet and tangy. I could eat this all day every day."

Her body felt like a live wire, electricity sparking through her system. It took all her concentration to follow orders and stay still because all she wanted to do was buck against his mouth, make him take more, go deeper.

He was a sadist. He was making her crazy. The man teased and taunted her with little licks and bites. His tongue moved over her labia and then brushed against her clitoris, nearly making her scream in frustration when he backed off.

"Is there something wrong, Deena?"

If he wanted her to beg, he would find out she was absolutely not above doing it if it got her what she wanted. Her whole body was taut with anticipation. Despite the lack of intimacy, the sex they'd had trained her to expect pleasure from him. In only a few short weeks of sleeping with Eric, she'd come to crave what he could give her. He wouldn't leave her unsatisfied. While it might be a fun game at times, Eric wasn't a bastard who took and gave nothing back.

"Please, Sir. Eric, I need to come. I need to feel your mouth on me."

"Tell me to fuck you with my tongue. Tell me you love it when I devour you."

"I do. I love it. It feels so good. Please fuck me with your tongue." The very act of saying the words, of hearing the way he growled them at her in that demanding Dom voice, got her even hotter. Every filthy word he said and commanded her to give back to him made her want more.

And he gave it to her. Without another word, he settled in and she felt the warm stroke of his tongue. He pierced her, diving deep inside while his thumb found her clitoris and started rubbing in circles. The rhythm seemed to follow the deep thrust of his tongue as he explored every inch of her pussy.

The wave hit her, making her call out and desperately clutch the headboard as the orgasm sped through her. Before she could even take a breath, he was up on his knees, reaching for a condom. He shoved his boxers off and started to roll the condom on his already hard cock.

Blood pounded through her, making her feel satiated and warm. She watched him through hooded eyes. His body was scarred and so beautiful it almost hurt to look at him. She wondered what he'd looked like before years of war had taken their toll. Likely softer, more boyish. The war had taken all the softness from Eric Vail's body and left nothing but rough man behind, but somehow it hadn't touched his soul. Though his body carried the scars, he was still open and kind and more than loving.

Did she even deserve a man like that?

The question whispered across her brain but she forgot it the minute he climbed on the bed with her. His big body was suddenly between her legs and she could feel his cock beginning to press in.

"Let go of the headboard. I want to feel your arms around me."

Because he never had. Because she'd been too scared. She'd been so selfish. She let go of her hold and let her arms drift around him as he started to work his way inside her body.

"This is what you taste like." He lowered his lips down to meet hers and she could taste her own essence there. His tongue plunged deep, sliding against hers as he thrust inside.

She would never get used to the feeling of that big cock stretching her. He was all around her, kissing and fucking and touching. This was what they'd been missing. She wrapped her legs around his waist, taking him deeper. She didn't want an inch of space between them.

"You feel so good," he groaned against her lips.

He was the one who felt good. Every thrust brought a spark of pleasure along her spine. She moved her hands along his back, loving the feel of his skin under her palm. His muscles moved as he worked over her. His cheek was against hers, letting her feel the rough stubble there. He was hard everywhere, his body flawed and amazing while the man himself could be so tender.

They were connected in a way they hadn't been before. She'd enjoyed the sex, but this meant so much more. She gave up trying to figure it out and let herself feel for once.

He shifted his hips and suddenly she couldn't think anymore. He hit a place deep inside her that made her whole body tighten.

"Eric." She breathed his name like a mantra as pleasure swept through her for the second time that night. Her body shuddered and she held on to him like he was the only real thing in the world.

He picked up the pace and kissed her while he found his own pleasure. His body shivered over hers and he held himself hard against her, pumping into her body.

Finally he relaxed, not bothering to disconnect their bodies. "That's what I wanted."

Deena lay there, her arms wrapped around him and wondered why she'd fought him at all.

CHAPTER NINE

"So do we need tickets to graduation?" Eric looked up from his prep work as Deena walked in. Luckily it was nothing more than cutting veggies. So very often she walked in as he was deboning a fish or prepping a side of beef. He didn't have to wash up before he touched her and that was a good thing since he found himself catching her as she threw herself into his arms.

Joy rushed through him. Yeah, he was going to need those tickets.

"I passed." Her arms squeezed him tight.

"All right!" Javi clapped and the line chefs all joined in.

"I'm so proud of you," he whispered in her ear. She'd done it. She'd pulled herself up and worked her ass off and she'd gotten her degree. Thank god one of them had. He was good at a couple of things, but sitting in a classroom wasn't one of them.

He settled her on her feet. She smiled at him like he was the only man on earth. It made those extra shifts he'd pulled for her completely worthwhile.

She grinned as she stepped back. "I am going to be a proud graduate of UT Dallas next Saturday. I know that the ceremony is in the middle of lunch service, but I hope a couple of you can make it."

He knew all about her graduation. He'd already made plans because he'd known damn straight his girl would pass that class. He and Tiffany and Ally were attending. Sean was stepping in when he would normally take the afternoon off and they were going to bring in a new server, who would eventually be replacing Deena. Everything was ready for him to attend and cheer her on. He'd spent a nice chunk of his savings buying her a new laptop. The one she was using had been purchased at a pawnshop and was at least five years out of date. The new one had all the bells and whistles she would need for her new job.

They were both starting new jobs in a few weeks. It worried him. They would be in the same town, but if she still wasn't willing to move a little on the no business talk edict, he could rapidly find himself playing second fiddle to her new job. She would have to work long hours. How long would it be before she'd made new friends and maybe going all the way into Dallas on club nights wouldn't be as compelling as it had been?

What happened when she realized he was always going to want her to work with him? That he felt like something would be missing without her?

There was time enough to worry about that later. For now he wanted to be happy. He was spending most nights with her. He'd even convinced her to stay at his place a couple of nights. It was so much easier since he believed in having food in the house and not living off yogurt and coffee. That girl was going to get a complete diet makeover when they moved in together.

He mentally backed away. It was something else to discuss at a later time. If there was a later time.

Tiffany worked her way around the large prep space and gave Deena a hug. "I'm so happy for you. No more classes."

Deena wrinkled her pretty nose. "Until I go for my MBA."

"Seriously?" Tiffany looked at her like she was insane.

Was she thinking of that? He could support her while she went to school. It would make sense for them to live together. It wasn't such a bad idea.

Deena shrugged. "I don't know. Probably not. I do know that I can use some of the money I won't be using on tuition to go shopping before I start my new job. Maybe not at your namesake, but I want to buy real clothes that no one else has worn before and that can't double as a work uniform. It's going to be so weird to have to figure out what to wear to work every day."

145

Because she'd worn her Top uniform for the last year, and before that it had been the uniform at whatever restaurant she happened to be working at. She was going to spread her wings and fly after years of being tied down first by a husband and then by debt.

Did he even have a right to try to tether her now?

"Guys, can I borrow the boss for a minute?" Deena asked, stepping close to Eric again.

Javi waved them off. "There's a nice closet in the front of house. I stash condoms in there and everything."

"I think we can go outside." There was no way he was taking Deena into Javier's broom closet.

Deena nodded. "Yes, I'm not missing graduation because I picked up a venereal disease, Javi."

"I'm very clean, sweetheart," Javi protested. "Did you hear about the condoms? I'm all about the glove love."

Tiffany groaned. "One of these days you're going to fall in love and she's going to be so turned off by your skanky reputation."

Javi shook his head. "Nah, this is too much man for any one woman. I owe it to the world to put this out there."

Eric took Deena's hand and led her outside. The sun was low in the sky, the heat of the day warming his skin. The back alley behind Top might contain the garbage bin, but it also had a basketball hoop and a couple of bistro tables and chairs for breaks.

"What did you need, baby?"

She went up on her toes and pressed a kiss against his lips. "To thank you. I don't know how I would have gotten through the last few weeks without you." She settled back on her feet.

"I was happy to help." He was also happy with how easily she touched him these days. "So do you have plans for after graduation or can I take you and Tiff and Ally to dinner?"

"It's going to be more than me and the girls. I'm going to need you to meet my mom." A grimace went over her face.

"Of course," he replied quickly. "Is that going to be a problem?"

"She doesn't exactly know you exist."

Yes, that was an issue. "And why is that? Because of the D/s relationship?"

"No, it's pretty much because you have a penis."

"Okay, that's something we're going to have to deal with. I was going to say we can certainly keep the fact that we're in a D/s relationship private, but your mom is going to figure out I probably have a penis. Is it my particular penis she'll take issue with or any penis at all?"

Deena sank into one of the chairs. "She's kind of a hard-core man-hater. I've told you about my father leaving. He took off and it was rough on her. I disappointed her when I got married so young. She's excited about me graduating. I think finding out that I've got a serious boyfriend is going to upset her."

He sat down across from her. They were serious? He'd always been serious. Hearing the word from her was a revelation. "I'll handle your mom."

"She can be difficult, Eric."

"And I can be charming."

"She won't like that one bit."

"Okay, then I'll be honest." He was planning on that anyway. He'd already thawed one frosty Holmes girl's heart. He could handle a second. Hey, maybe after a few decades, they would both figure out he wasn't going anywhere.

"Whatever she says, don't take it too personally," Deena said with a frown. "She's spent a lot of years hating my dad. When Eddie and I got divorced, she tried to get me to move back in with her because, as she put it, we didn't need men. We just needed each other. I wasn't willing to go back to small town life. We haven't talked much over the last couple of years. I'm a little surprised she's willing to come to the graduation."

"She's proud of you for rising above it all," he guessed. He hoped. If she was coming to Dallas to try to talk her daughter into going home, Momma should be prepared for a fight. He wasn't going to let go of her easily.

Deena nodded. "I'm going with that theory, too. Anyway, she's staying in a hotel downtown. Another surprise. My mom tends to be super frugal, so I expected her to sleep on my couch."

"That would definitely be awkward if we're trying to hide the fact that I have a penis."

A throaty laugh came out of her mouth, the sound going straight to his cock. That closet was looking better and better.

"We can't hide your penis, babe. We do have to talk about the fact that we're supposed to graduate from training school a few days before my college graduation, and one of us is going to have to tell Big Tag that we're only going to play together. I heard a rumor that he's planning on pimping the new Doms out." Her eyes had narrowed and got that steely glint she always used when she was going to be stubborn.

"I've got Macon working on that end." He wasn't about to tell Big Tag that his pimping plan wasn't going to work out unless he had a pie to give him. "Don't worry about it. I'll handle Big Tag. I'm not about to top that crazy chick from the DA's office. Besides, I happen to know we're the only ones coming out of this thing as a couple. Althea has agreed to work full time for Sanctum."

Deena's eyes went wide. "Are you serious? Doesn't that mean she can't have sex?"

It was a juicy bit of gossip. "Not while she's working with clients, she can't. I listened to that lecture when Big Tag offered us the jobs. That man really likes the word fuck."

"He offered you a job?" The question came out quietly, but he could hear the shock in her voice. And that little tone told him he was back firmly in boyfriend territory and that he shouldn't head into Dom mode. It was a delicate balance with her, but he wouldn't have it any other way.

"He's looking for dungeon monitors and some professionals. The club has taken on a life of its own. I get the feeling if he could take it back to its roots, he would, but Big Tag is a realist. McKay-Taggart needs the connections he's made through the club. He's got all the high rollers in Dallas and some national connections coming in and out of Sanctum. He can use that when the going gets tough, and it always does. He's building an empire."

"That doesn't mean you have to be his soldier."

He reached out and put a hand over hers. "I'm not. I've agreed to be a dungeon monitor, but not to professionally top clients. Javier, Althea, and Gage are all going to do that. I suspect he's going to have a talk with the subs about the same types of jobs. I saw the new girl had already signed a contract, the one who got paired with Javier."

"Mia?" Deena's fingers tangled with his. "She's nice. A bit weird though. She asks a lot of questions."

The pretty blonde had been a mystery to Javi. He'd done everything he could to get in the girl's panties, but she constantly turned him down. With a smile, of course. "She's agreed to work at Sanctum full time so he's got plenty of new recruits. He won't be too upset about us."

"Good, because there's something else we need to talk about and it does involve Big Tag. And Chef. I looked into your business plan."

It was the day for surprises. "You did?"

"Yes, and after we discuss that I have a surprise for you." She let go of his hand and reached down into her bag, pulling out a familiar file folder. It was the same printout he'd given her days before. His business plan. He was surprised when she pulled out the contract he was set to sign with the Taggart brothers.

He frowned down at it. "Where did you get that?"

"You left it on the kitchen table along with the business plan. I assumed you wanted me to look at everything if I'm going to help you with this." She flipped through the contract. "I made a few changes, but I think it's sound. I want to talk to the lawyer about a couple of things. I think the royalty fee is a little high."

He winced. "It's Sean's company and his brand. He and Ian are helping me start up. The fee isn't outside the norm."

"I know that, but I'm trying to look out for your best interests. And it's on the high end of normal. It also ties you up for the next five years."

Did she think he hadn't read the contract? "I'm cool with it. I'm not going anywhere."

"No. You won't be for five years," she pointed out needlessly. "According to this you can't open another restaurant for five years. As far as I can tell, you can't even work in another restaurant for five years."

"I'll be working at my own, Deena." He wasn't sure what the problem was and he didn't like the tone of her voice.

"What happens if it doesn't work out in Fort Worth?" She leaned forward, pointing to the contract. "Anything can happen. We should know that. We got hit by a tornado last year. What if that happens at your location? What if the city comes in and uses eminent domain to push you out of your location? Any of a number of things can happen. There's no language excluding failure in this contract. If Sean wanted to hold you to the noncompete clause, you wouldn't be able to work in the industry even if your place of business fails. You would be forced to move to another city and start all over again."

He sighed. She was being cynical. "That wasn't the intent of the language."

"The intent means nothing in a court of law," she pointed out. "This contract binds you even if something happens to Sean and someone else takes over."

The whole conversation was making him antsy. This wasn't what he'd meant for her to do when he'd asked her to look at his business plan. He hadn't meant for her to go through the contract. He simply wanted to open a damn restaurant. He wasn't going to make a federal case out of it.

She sat up straighter, obviously warming to her subject. "I also don't like that there's no written agreement that forces Sean to support the restaurant with personal appearances. He's about to be on TV. Food Network is doing a special on new chefs and Sean Taggart is going to be featured. Chef is smart, funny, and quite frankly the man is gorgeous. He's going to be very popular on that show. Six months from now, it's not only the Top brand that will be worth money. It's going to be Chef Taggart, and if he's making money off your hard work, he can support it with guaranteed appearances. It would also be nice if we could get you featured on the show. You've got a great backstory. We can use that with the press."

This was the part of the job he hated. He wanted to cook. That was all he wanted to do, but he could see the point. Still, it didn't seem right to ask the man to do more than what he'd already done. "I think Top Fort Worth can stand on its own and I don't even want to talk about the press. That will work itself out."

She shook her head. "It won't. I want to talk to you about bringing in a publicist. Not full time at first. I have a couple of names of people I want to interview. If we can get some solid write-ups about the way Top works, I think we can draw great crowds. I expect that you're going to continue hiring veterans like Sean has."

"Of course." It was part of their business model. They brought in vets who struggled to find work and if they showed promise, trained them to cook or to manage. But that had nothing to do with publicity. "I'm not hiring a publicist. We don't need one."

She continued talking like he hadn't said a word. "I also want to talk about community outreach. Fort Worth has some great events I think we should be involved in. Main Street Arts Festival, there's a yearly restaurant night at the zoo."

He held up a hand. "Stop. This is too much for me."

"I know it's a lot, but it's okay because I'm handling it for you. I'm going to talk to Chef about my plan. I think he's going to see the value."

"Deena, did you hear a word I said?"

"I did and I think you're wrong. What I'm proposing is best for you, and in the end it's best for Sean. He's taking a cut of your profits. He should want that cut to be as high as possible."

"Or he could expect me to work my ass off and do it on my own," he argued. She might have been the one to go to class, but it was his butt on the line.

"Then why call it Top at all? Why not open your own place?"

"Because I don't have the money to open my own place." He forced himself to stop because he'd barked those words at her. She was calling him out on a bunch of stuff he didn't want to hear. "I'm sorry, baby. I don't think you understand what I'm trying to do."

"Yes, I do. You're devaluing yourself," she shot back.

Eric took a deep breath, measuring his words. "I'm not. I'm taking a very good offer and running with it. That's all I'm doing. You're trying to make things complicated because you just graduated and that's what you've been taught to do."

"No, I've been taught how to run a business. I've been taught how to read a contract and how to negotiate. You're the one who asked me to look into this." Confusion settled over her features.

"I wanted you to check my business plan. To run my numbers not question my business decisions. I didn't ask you to do that at all," he corrected. "I certainly didn't ask you to come in here and try to convince me that the best deal I've gotten in my life is really a way for a man I trust to screw me over."

Her face flushed. "I wasn't trying to say you were getting screwed, Eric. Look, I understand where you're coming from. It's hard to ask for the things we deserve."

He felt his fists clench, frustration rising. This wasn't the conversation he'd intended to have with her this afternoon. "You have no idea where I'm coming from and I do deserve this restaurant."

"You're willfully misunderstanding me."

He pushed back from the table, unable to remain sitting. "And you're accusing a man I respect of trying to fuck me over."

"He's not trying to screw you," Deena replied. "He's only looking to make the best deal he can for himself and Top. This is the business world, Eric. It's not the Navy. You don't have to take what you're given. You can demand more."

"Or I can be grateful for what I've been given." How did he get her to understand that not everything had to be a fight?

"You haven't been given anything. You earned it."

It was obvious that she was never going to understand. "I am not having this discussion with you. You said you wanted to keep our business and personal lives separate. If you're going to behave like this, maybe we should."

"Behave like what? Like I have an opinion?" She stood up, picking up her purse and slinging it over her shoulder. "I will make certain not to give you an opinion again. I have to wonder if you didn't want my business advice, why did you want me as an advisor?"

"Like I said before, I wanted you to look at my plan."

She stared him straight in the eye, her gaze holding his. "Your plan is flawed because your contract is flawed. You'll fail or you'll end up being mediocre because you don't believe in yourself or you would walk in and ask Sean for the things you need to make the restaurant great."

That was a kick in the gut. "I'm going to fail now? Because I don't listen to you?"

She stepped back, turning toward the door. "Like I said, maybe you won't fail, but you're definitely not stepping up for yourself. I learned the hard way that I have to watch out for my best interests. I have to believe in myself and value myself because no one else will. You didn't want a business partner, Eric. You want someone to do the work you aren't interested in. You want someone to keep the books and tell you how fabulous you're doing."

"Well, it's obvious to me you don't think much of me at all," he replied, bitterness in his gut.

She shook her head. "You haven't listened to a word I've said. Or maybe you have and you simply don't value it. I'm glad I found out before I did something stupid. I have to go get ready for my shift."

"That's a good idea. All we're going to do right now is argue."

Without another look back, she stepped inside. The door closed behind her.

She was wrong about him. He did want a partner, but he certainly didn't want one who questioned the motivations of everyone in his life.

"Wow, that went like shit, man," a deep voice said. Sean stepped out. "Sorry, I park back here. I wasn't trying to listen in, but damn, you two got loud at the end."

Fuck and double fuck. "I wish you hadn't heard that. She doesn't mean what she says. She's trying to prove herself. You know how it is. College students think they know everything even when they're heading into their thirties."

"I think she meant it." Sean had his white jacket thrown over his shoulder. He put a hand in his pocket and pulled his cell phone out. "And don't discount the Ivory Tower faction. Sometimes they pay more attention to details than the rest of us do." He pushed a button and put the phone to his ear. "Mitch, you motherfucker. Are fucking kidding me? You put him in a noncompete clause for five years? Have you lost your damn brain?" There was a pause. "I told you what I wanted. Two years and we reevaluate." There was another pause and then Sean cursed. "I don't care about starting places. We're not negotiating this. Keep your wiggle room to yourself. Redo the clause before you get here. I don't care if you're on your way. Have Laurel fax a new one." He hung up the phone. "Damn lawyers. Mitch Bradford is a personal friend, but I swear to god I wouldn't want to be the one on the opposite side of the table from him. I'm fairly certain he learned bargaining from Satan himself."

"The contract is fine." He'd read it. He wasn't absolutely certain what was normal in this case, but he wasn't about to argue with…

He'd been about to think of Sean as his CO.

Sean frowned at him. "It's not fine and Deena was absolutely right. This should be a negotiation. I've been lazy about letting Mitch handle it up to this point because I've had a lot going on, and quite frankly after what happened with…well, it's been easier to focus on cooking and being with my family. I'm sorry. I'll take a look at the contract again. Mitch always goes after the best deal for his client even if it means screwing someone else. Tell me you took his advice and you've got your own lawyer coming in this afternoon."

At least he could be honest about that. He glanced over to the door that Deena had disappeared through and wondered what she was doing. Likely cursing his name. "Yeah, though I haven't actually met with her. I was supposed to the other day, but we had the problem with the menu and I ended up changing our scallop dish to halibut. It's going to be fine. I'm sitting down to talk with her in a few minutes and I'll sign the contract after that."

Was he doing exactly what Deena accused him of? Was he treating this like he was still in the military and his CO was giving him a promotion? In the Navy, one didn't negotiate promotions. One earned it and hoped his CO noticed.

This wasn't the military.

"Or you'll sit down and tell me what you need to make the contract work," Sean said, his voice soft. "Do you think I haven't been where you are? That I don't know how hard this is on you? You went into the Navy as a kid, right?"

Now he was seeing how easy it was to stay in that mentality. Sean wasn't his CO. Sean was about to be his business partner, and that meant Eric had to be a good one. "Yeah. Straight out of high school. Before that I worked at my dad's sporting goods store during summers. All I've known is the Navy and kitchens since then. I guess the business stuff freaks me out a little."

"Then it's very good that your girl has a business head on her shoulders. She's spot on. I don't like to think about the Food Network show. It seems a little douchey to me."

"Then why do it?"

"Grace," Sean admitted. "She told me if I didn't take this opportunity I would regret it for the rest of my life. It's a chance to grow this business, to build something for our daughter, for our friends. I don't want to be a TV chef, but if I can talk about what happens when vets leave the military, about how hard it is to find yourself after years of service, maybe I should. And I owe everything to my girls. They deserve the best life I can give them. So I'll go on TV. You need to figure out what you want and do it quickly, brother."

"I want to open Top Fort Worth."

"I wasn't talking about that. I was talking about with Deena. Do you want a sub or a queen? Don't think I'm saying one is better than the other. They're simply different, and every man has to decide what he needs in his life. Every Dom I know has been forced to ask himself the question and there's no right answer. If you'll be happy with a woman who is submissive to you in every way and you have her best interests at heart, then you should go for it. I don't think Deena's that girl. Do you know why I want Grace to submit to me in the club and the bedroom?"

Eric knew the answer to that question. He'd been around Grace Taggart long enough that the answer came easily. "She won't do it anywhere else."

"Exactly. Grace is my queen and we run this business, our family, and our lives together. I don't get anywhere close to this place without that woman by my side. Deena could be a queen, but you have to stuff your pride down long enough to listen to her, really listen to her, and let her lead when you can't. It's hard to admit that we don't know it all."

"Nope, I know nothing about this," he said quickly. His gut knotted at the thought of what he'd done to her. "I wanted it to be easy. I didn't want to fuck a good thing up and so I wasn't listening to her. I was listening to my fear, and we all know where that can get us."

Sean put a hand on his shoulder. "Go talk to her. Grovel a little, maybe."

He could do that. Pride was important, but Deena meant more. "Thanks, and I'll talk to the lawyer. We might need to iron a few things out."

Sean opened the door to the kitchen. "I might need to talk to Deena about some of the things she was advising you on. Hell, maybe

I'll hire her."

"Not on your life, Chef. That's my queen." And he was keeping her.

Sean smiled as Eric strode through the door. "We're at Code Red, gentlemen."

"Thank god." Big Tag was leaning against the counter, his arms crossed over his massive chest. "I thought it was all going to be boring lawyer stuff."

"Shit," Javi said. "I knew something was wrong when Deena ran through here. What did you do?"

Eric winced. It was so great to have a damn audience. Code Red was Chef's sarcastic way to let everyone know there was relationship drama happening. "I'll fix it."

He had to. He jogged through the door and prayed she hadn't left.

* * * *

Deena pushed through the locker room in a haze of tears.

Asshole. Jerk. He was exactly like every other man in her damn life. Useless and uncaring and now she'd wrecked her whole life again and over a man. It was inconceivable. What the hell had she been thinking?

"Whoa, that is a serious face." Charlotte Taggart was sitting on the sofa, a tablet in her hands. "Sorry, the girls are with Alex and Eve for a few hours. I came with Ian to sign the paperwork for your boyfriend's restaurant. I want to make sure Mitch doesn't try to screw Eric. Don't take it personally. Mitch tries to screw everyone. It's part of what makes him an awesome lawyer. I was just catching up on some reading. I can leave if you need me to."

Deena was fairly certain Charlotte Taggart didn't get a ton of alone time, much less reading time. She had twins and a job and was active in club life.

So she would suck it up and get through dinner shift and then try to figure out what the hell she was going to do with the rest of her stupid life. "No problem. Read away. I'll be out of your hair in a minute or two."

Charlotte set down the tablet. "I think we're going to the same place. Is it wrong to drink during negotiations? Because the bartender here makes a mean martini and I usually find these things hella boring. It was easier in the mob. Don't like the terms of a contract? Shoot 'em between the eyes and take over their territory. Bloodier, but easier and with a lot less arguing and ten-dollar words."

Charlotte had a colorful background. "Don't worry about it. I happen to know that there will be no negotiations. Eric is planning on bending over and taking it any way he can get it. And I won't be there to watch. I've got menus to print and my replacement to train."

And no job since she'd called the firm earlier today and explained she'd changed her mind and was going a different direction. She'd intended to tell Eric that she was accepting his crappy, nearly no upfront pay offer because she was dumb and in love and believed in him.

What the hell had she been thinking?

"Whoa, what's going on? Is there trouble in paradise?" Charlotte asked.

The door to the locker room swung open and Tiffany raced in. "I heard there was a Code Red. Who is it? I asked Sebastian but he said he wouldn't lower himself to discuss gossip. Seriously? What is wrong with that man? Is it Jenni? Because I met her new guy and he had one of those weird pencil beards that takes dudes like four hours to perfect. He's got to be a douche. Oh, hello, Mrs. Taggart."

"Charlotte, please," the redhead said. "And I'm fairly certain it isn't douche beard. I think perfect Eric might have fucked up."

Tiffany's jaw dropped. "No."

This was why she didn't get super close to people. Because it was embarrassing. It was humiliating.

Why? She stopped in the middle of buttoning up her shirt. "Why am I embarrassed?"

"I have no idea, but I'm looking forward to finding out," Charlotte replied. "I've already read that book a couple of times. This is better."

Deena's first instinct was to push them all away and hide the pain, but why should she? She wasn't the one at fault here. "He's being a massive ass."

"Eric the Gallant?" Tiffany shook her head. "Don't tell him I called him that, but he reminds me of a knight sometimes. What did he do?"

"I tried to give him very good business advice and he basically told me to shut up. He used more polite words, but he said I didn't know what I was talking about."

"Rude. Does he have a degree in business?" Tiffany asked. "No. You wouldn't tell him how to cook."

"It's worse." It felt good to talk about it. "You know that job I took? The dream job with the nice salary, benefits, and paid health insurance? Yeah, I quit that to become Eric's business manager because I am that stupid."

Tiffany's eyes widened. "Honey, this is not like it was before. You can talk to Eric. And we can call the company back. Maybe the job is still open."

Deena took a deep breath. "No, it won't be. Hell, I wouldn't take me back, either. I'm going to take a few days and reassess my situation. I might talk to Chef. I have some ideas about restaurant publicity. Maybe I can consult with him."

"Or you can come in and talk about rehabbing McKay-Taggart's image. We've run into some trouble after Ian got pissed at a rival firm and sent the managing director a big box of glitter dildos," Charlotte said. "He rigged it so they blew up and went all over the dude's office. We're getting sued for glitter injuries, and one of the flying dicks might have poked an eye. In Ian's defense, that asshole screwed up two of our operations in Africa and ended up getting Liam briefly kidnapped by a rebel army. He's totally fine. Li bought them all whiskey and escaped after they'd partied too hard, but Ian felt like a little revenge. Guy can't take a joke. I mean that literally. His name really is Guy."

"Yeah, I will look into that for you." It appeared she needed to find a good publicist for all of the people around her.

Charlotte stood up. "Don't give up on Eric so easily. He's scared, Deena. When guys get scared they turn into massive tools. Women, we tend to grab a bottle of wine and talk it over with our friends, but guys get difficult."

"Well, he can be difficult all he wants. I won't try to help him again. He made himself very plain." She was going to be calm. Hey, at least they weren't living together like she'd been planning on suggesting. She hadn't fully tied her life to a man who didn't really want her. That was a plus. She could save her dignity and be pleasant with him and he didn't ever have to know what she'd almost done.

She worked the buttons of her shirt, trying to smooth out the wrinkles.

"You made yourself plain," Tiffany said quietly. "It didn't stop him."

Deena turned. Both Tiffany and Charlotte were watching her. "What is that supposed to mean?"

Tiffany took a few seconds but seemed to come to some conclusion. "It means you're a pain in the ass and he still wanted you."

She could handle the pain in the ass part. Tiff was right about that. To say she'd been difficult at the beginning of their relationship was an understatement. "I accept that but he doesn't want me now. I think he's one of those guys who likes the chase. Now that he's got me, he doesn't want the same thing from me and I can't be the girl he seems to need."

"Whoa, that is some nice deflection there, Holmes." Charlotte clapped her hands together. "You're good at this."

Maybe she wouldn't be working for McKay-Taggart. "I didn't ask for your opinion."

Charlotte nodded. "No one ever does. It's a real mistake because I'm super good at this. Kai and Eve might be the ones with the fancy degrees, but I'm the one who deflected for years and you can't even come close to me, little girl."

"What the hell am I supposed to be deflecting?"

"Oh, I think you're good at deflecting everything. Emotions. Friendships. Definitely relationships."

"I was trying to have a relationship with Eric."

"And the minute Mr. Perfect wasn't so perfect, you ended it," Charlotte pointed out. "I would bet he doesn't even know you're ending it. He's probably out there waiting for you to walk out so he can talk to you because he feels bad. What's your plan when he walks up to you and puts his arms around you?"

She'd already thought of it. She'd seen it play through in her mind. He would feel bad, but she knew the real Eric now and she wouldn't buy it. When he tried to touch her, she would walk away, tell him she wasn't ready and then she would stop answering his calls, stop seeing him, move on.

Like she'd always done. Walk away because it was easier than working things out.

Charlotte didn't wait for her to answer. "You plan on shutting him out, but that's a mistake. Once you start down that road, there's not a lot of going back. Not for someone like you. Tell me something. How long would it have been before you stopped answering Tiffany's calls? Your friends from the club's?"

Charlotte was getting to her. She didn't like the antsy feeling in her gut. How many times had she walked away? How many times had she watched her mom do it?

"I don't know. It's…I've never had friends like this before and sometimes I don't know how to trust any of this." She felt tears welling. "My mom and I moved a lot. We did it because we would run out of money or she would need a fresh start. I was always the new kid until I met Eddie. I felt like the new kid here until I got together with Eric."

"They're not the same," Tiffany insisted. "Not even close. I think Charlotte is right. Eric is being an ass because he's scared about this deal. He wants it badly and he's afraid to do anything to mess it up. Neither one of you is trusting the people around you to have your backs. I'm your friend, D. I'm going to be your friend whether you ever call me again because I decided a long time ago that's who I am. This is your moment. Who are you? Are you the woman who lets a guy like Eric go because he's a dumbass? Or are you woman enough to fight back?"

There was a knock on the door and then she heard Eric's voice. "Hey, Deena, sweetheart, can I come in?"

She went to the door and threw the bolt. "I'll be out in a minute."

Tiffany sighed. "This is a mistake, D. He's not your ex-husband."

"I know that," she admitted. She still needed the safety of that door between them because she wasn't sure of what to do. If Eric walked in here, would she dissolve into a puddle of submissive goo at his feet? "At least I know it in my head. My heart is a little slower. I need a minute because I'm mad at him right now."

There was another knock followed by a male voice. "Yo, Charlie, Mitch and the other lawyer are here. Let's get this thing done and we might still be able to make out in Sean's office before we have to pick up the girls."

That got Charlotte moving. "Excuse me. That man knows how to make out. I hope you get your shit together, Holmes, because Eric needs a partner. The thing is partners argue and fight and then they make out in a convenient space. Well, it's what people in love do anyway."

People in love. Was she in love with Eric?

Charlotte opened the door and before it could close again, Eric was walking through. His face dropped the minute he saw her.

"Baby, I am so sorry."

Was she going to walk away because he'd been a dick? He would probably be a dick again because underneath all that Captain America awesomeness he was a man with flaws and fears. And she was a woman with the same.

Her father had walked out on someone he'd claimed to love. He hadn't stayed. Hadn't fought. It finally struck her that she'd misused the word. Her father hadn't loved her. Fathers who loved their kids didn't walk out on them. Husbands who loved their wives didn't throw in the towel and find a new life. There hadn't been love. Not from her father. Not from her husband. Eric wasn't sitting somewhere waiting to see if she would take his abuse, planning on how to use her. He'd been an ass and he was standing right here in front of her, his handsome face so earnest it brought tears to her eyes.

"Do you love me?"

"Yes." He said the word without hesitation. His hands came up to frame her face as he stared down at her. "Oh, baby, I've loved you for a long time but I was afraid to say it because I know how you feel about it. I know you won't trust it."

But she trusted him. It was a decision like anything else. She'd decided to move on with her life when she'd signed up for college. Wasn't this a choice, too? To move on with him? "I love you, too."

His jaw dropped. "Are you serious? Deena, I'm sorry about the way I talked to you. I didn't mean to make you feel like I don't respect your opinions."

"But you did. You were a condescending asshole and if you do it again, we're going to fight. So you need to sit back and let me do my job. I better have a job because I quit the one I had."

"You did what?"

It was good to know she could surprise him. "I quit my job so I can run the business end of the restaurant and I think we should save money by moving in together, but first I'm going out and making sure you don't sign that contract until it's right. If you want to fight, we can find somewhere to fight, but I'm going to make you see reason because you're worth more than what they're offering."

His lips curled up and his hands moved in front of his chest. "Go for it, baby. This is all you. Where I come from men cook dinner and women deal with the lawyers. By the way, mine is here. Her name is something Jensen. I don't know. I haven't actually talked to her yet. You can do that. Right?"

Too much. Too much emotion. Too much stimulation. Way too much coincidence. "Renee Jensen?"

Tiffany gasped. She knew that name.

Eric nodded. "Yes. I think that's her name. Mitch brought her in from another firm. Why? Is she bad?"

Oh, she was a bitch, all right. There was a time when Deena might have hidden away and hoped that her past didn't catch up to her, but today was not that day. She might technically be walking across a stage on Saturday, but today was freaking graduation day. It was time to jump in the deep end and be the woman she wanted to be.

"She's fired is what she is." Deena threw open the door and stepped out into the hallway, her mind on one thing.

It was her night to take out the trash.

"Okay." Eric was right behind her. "Is there a particular reason we're firing her?"

She must have looked as purpose driven as she felt because Javier practically jumped out of the way as she rounded the corner.

"Do we have anything worse than a Code Red?" Javi asked.

"I don't know. I'm not even sure why we're firing the lawyer we haven't met yet," Eric admitted. "But she's in charge. I'm just here for the ride."

Tiffany was hurrying along behind them. "That's her ex-husband's new girlfriend. The one he left her for."

"I'm going to kill Mitch," Eric swore.

And there she was. Renee Jensen was dressed in a perfect business suit, her dark hair cut in a chic bob, every inch of her face cosmetically enhanced. She leaned over, talking to Mitch Bradford. The big guy in the suit came in for lunch at least once a week. He usually came with his wife and their baby son. Luckily today he was alone, which was good because babies didn't need to watch their fathers get an asskicking. A verbal one at least.

But first she was going to deal with Renee.

The brunette skank ho turned, her eyes widening in surprise. "Oh my god, is that Deena? Are you working here?" Her lips curled in a snarky grin. "Can you get me a coffee? Two sugars."

Mitchell frowned as he looked up at her. "Deena? Are you all right?"

She picked up Renee's probably thousand-dollar briefcase and turned on her heels. "I will be fine once I deal with your shitty contract, but I'm not doing anything with her in my space."

"Hey, what are you doing with my briefcase?" Renee started to stalk after her in those five-inch heels of hers.

"You are fired. I'm Eric Vail's business manager and you are never going to be his lawyer," she said as she approached the door, opened it, and tossed the briefcase straight out and almost into the street. "Get the hell out of here and don't come back. These are my people."

"You bitch." She ran out to grab her briefcase.

Deena took the opportunity to lock the door. She could hear Renee start to knock and scream, but Deena simply turned back to Mitch. "You have terrible taste in lawyers."

Mitch nodded. "She was simply doing a favor for her boss, Deena. I was unaware of her…" He leaned over and Charlotte whispered something in his ear. He nodded. "Sorry, I was unaware of her status as a complete skank. I will, naturally, bring in another, less skanky attorney."

Sean sighed and sat down before yelling toward the bar. "Sebastian, screw the wine. We're going to need some Scotch."

Eric slipped his hand into hers. "Yes, we're going to need that because Deena and I have some problems we would like to work out. You want to explain the situation to them?"

All eyes were on her and she kind of wished she'd tucked her shirt in. It didn't matter. All that mattered was the fact that she was here with him.

She nodded and began to speak.

CHAPTER TEN

Eric looked out at the stage. He was nervous. He was actually nervous about this. It was odd because it was all he'd been able to think about for the last few days. What if she changed her mind? What was he going to do if she turned tail and ran?

Go after her. Bring her home. It was what he would always do with this woman.

"Are you sure you want to do this?" Big Tag asked. "Because sometimes playing the field is fun. Think about all those women you could be fucking."

Eric rolled his eyes because he'd spent enough time with Big Tag to know when he was being an asshole in order to diffuse an emotional situation. "You said if I took the Dom in residence job I couldn't fuck the clients."

Tag's eyes rolled right back. "Yeah, because so many of you listen to me about that. I promise every one of the new hires will be screwing someone they shouldn't within weeks. I would crack down on it, but hey, I kind of like the drama. Your girl created some nice drama the other day, by the way."

He couldn't help but smile. Deena had fought for him and she'd won. Though Big Tag had moaned and complained about every concession, Eric was pretty sure it had all been for show. "She did what she needed to do."

"I loved it when she called the cops on the skanky lawyer chick because she wouldn't go away. That's the only reason I'm condoning this ceremony of yours. I like a chick with balls. Not real balls, of course. Remind me to tell you about an assignment I had in Thailand some time. Yeah, that was not what I expected." Big Tag clapped him on the back. "Good luck out there. Hope she says yes."

Eric sighed and followed him out to the stage where Deena was already standing. Every bit of his nerves fell away. He had to stop and take a breath because she was stunning in an emerald and black corset and leather boy shorts. One day he was going to get her in a wedding gown. He'd already decided that there was no way he was eloping. He wanted all the ceremony he could get with this woman. His woman.

But for today, she was perfect.

"Welcome, everyone," Big Tag said, addressing the crowd. "We're here today to witness the formal bonding of a submissive to her Master. It sucks because they both promised me they wouldn't take this shit seriously in any way and they intended to sleep around as much as they possibly could, but once again all my plans are foiled." He turned serious, his face going a bit grave. "I started Sanctum as a place to play, a place where my friends could blow off some steam. Like all things in life, it's grown and evolved and hopefully it's aging well. It's also become a place where more than one of you has found the person you needed to feel complete. Though we've lost some along the way, we're still here and I'm very happy to bring these two together, to make our family a little bigger. I can joke about it all I like, but the truth is we can never have too much family. Eric, tonight I grant you Master rights here at Sanctum. Deena, I welcome you as well. Is this the man you wish to submit to? Can you respect him and his place here? Will you do your utmost to ensure his happiness and comfort?"

"I will be properly submissive when I'm in this club and a kick ass partner out of it," Deena said with a grin.

Big Tag leaned in. "That means she'll kick your ass. Trust me. I know. All the good ones do."

"I can handle that," Eric assured him.

Big Tag clapped his hands together. "All right then, Master Eric, is this the woman you want to be responsible for? Will you take care of her and do your utmost to ensure her happiness and comfort? Will you protect her and honor her place here?"

He was not going to get choked up. He wasn't. Maybe he should rethink the eloping thing because he might make an idiot of himself at a wedding. He reached for her hand, the weight of it comforting to him. "I will be properly dominant when I'm in this club and our bedroom and I will be a kick ass partner out of it. I love you, baby. Will you accept this necklace as a sign that we belong together? As a promise of things to come?"

There were tears in her eyes when she nodded.

He pulled out the Cartier necklace he'd saved up for a long time to buy. This was the right woman, the one he would be with for the rest of his days.

He placed the necklace around her throat and kissed her as their friends cheered.

Big Tag nodded. "All right, that's enough mushy shit. There's a reception in the bar and Sanctum is open for play."

Receptions were awesome, but he wasn't going to this one. He leaned over, hooking an arm under Deena's knees and the other around her back. He lifted her up. "Have fun everyone."

"Yeah, I thought that's what you'd do," Big Tag said as his wife joined him. "Privacy room two is fully stocked and ready for you. Have fun." He put an arm around his wife. "Kiss me, baby. You know I get emotional at these things."

Charlotte smiled up at him. "I know you do. And privacy room number one is all set up for us."

If he didn't get a move on, he would have to fight Big Tag to get up the stairs, and that was not going to happen.

"Hey, we're missing our reception," Deena complained, but snuggled in his arms as he started up the stairs to the privacy rooms.

"I will have them send up a plate later," he replied. "You'll need your strength."

"I bet I will."

He loved the way the necklace looked around her throat. Maybe it made him a caveman but he wanted the world to know this woman was his. She'd chosen him. She stood by him. It was all a man needed to make his way in the world—a woman who loved him.

The door was slightly open as though whoever had set it up had known the man using it wouldn't have his hands free. It was nice to know they were joining a long line of loving couples here at Sanctum. He lightly kicked the door open. The room was lit with candles. There was a big bed complete with a bondage package he intended to use later, but first, he had plans for his sub.

He set her on her feet and then locked the door. "Take the clothes off and find your position."

"Not playing around, are we?" Deena asked in a husky voice, her hands already tugging at the front hooks of her corset.

"Not tonight. Tonight, I'm in charge. I loved the way you handled Mitch and I adored watching you take care of business the other day, but the whole time all I could think about was getting you here and making you mine. Tomorrow, you get to be the graduate. The day after, you get to be the Top franchise's ballsy business manager, but tonight, oh baby, tonight you are going to be my sweet submissive."

She practically glowed when she smiled at him. He'd been a bit jealous at first when Sean had suggested Deena take over for both restaurants. He wanted to keep her all to himself, but he was rapidly finding joy in watching her spread her wings and fly. His girl was too smart, too ambitious for just one restaurant. She would help them build an empire. "I can do that for you, Master."

No more Sirs. He was her Master now and he would always honor her. "Show me your breasts."

She managed to tug the final eyelet off, freeing her breasts. She tossed the corset on the chair beside her. Eric was certain that chair was built for bondage as well, but it would serve a different purpose tonight.

She stood in front of him, skin soft and lovely in the candlelight. Her hair flowed around her shoulders and her breasts…oh, her breasts made his mouth water.

"The rest of it," he demanded. He got to be demanding here. He was more than willing to let her handle all the business negotiations she wanted as long as he got to dominate her here. This was the place where he could bring her pleasure and comfort and joy. This was the place where he could find his own. With her and only her.

She placed her shoes and the boy shorts she'd been wearing on the dresser top along with the corset before moving in front of him and sinking gracefully to her knees. Her head dropped in a submissive manner, her palms up on her thighs.

He wanted to feel her mouth on him before he moved on to the more exotic time of the evening. Eric stepped in front of her. She was so lovely in this pose, calm and tranquil and waiting his order. She trusted him. It was an enormous leap of faith because her trust had been destroyed before. How much courage had it taken for her to open herself to him, to let him in?

He reached down, gently lifting her chin so he could look her in the eyes. "I love you, Deena. I will never make you sorry you're here with me."

"And I'll never make you sorry you were patient with me," she replied serenely.

He wouldn't be. His patience had brought him her and that was all he could ask for. Well, actually he could think of a few other things he could ask for. "Undo my leathers."

Her lips curved up in a sultry smile as her hands came up, reaching for the ties on his leathers and gracefully undoing them. His dick was already hard as a rock and desperate for her affection. He hissed as she took it into her hand. Damn but no matter how many times he made love to this woman it always felt like this, like he was young and learning the joys of a woman all over again. She made him feel this way.

"Kiss it." He couldn't stop the low growl in his tone.

Her eyes were up, looking at him as she leaned forward and brushed her lips against the head of his cock. Pure fire swept through him as she ran the flat of her tongue around his dick.

"That's what I want, but don't think you'll take me all the way. You're not getting off that easy. Not at all. Tonight I'm going to have everything I've wanted. Everything I've been preparing you for."

Her eyes widened and she moved back on her heels. "We should talk about that."

Nope. He wasn't playing that way tonight. "You'll love it. You have no problem going for hours with the plug. Don't even pretend. You've started to like it."

She leaned forward again. "I can cry and plead if it makes you happy."

He wasn't a sadist, though he did like to play with her. "Not tonight. Tonight I want to make you come. I want to take that pretty ass and make it mine."

She licked at him, drawing her tongue over the slit of his cock and sucking at the little drop of moisture there. "Everything I have is yours, Master."

And she would get everything from him. He would work his hardest to build something special with her, to have a life they could both be proud of. He wound a hand in the silk of her hair and drew her forward. She shivered as he pulled slightly. He'd learned exactly the right amount of pressure to apply to ensure she was wet and ready for him.

He twisted her hair, tugging lightly, and was rewarded with a moan. The sound moved over his sensitive flesh. Deena leaned over, taking more of him. He watched as his dick disappeared between those gorgeous lips. Her tongue moved over and around his stalk, and he wasn't going to think about anything but how good it felt.

"Take more." He forced another inch in, hissing as her teeth lightly scratched over him. "Don't make me spank you. I'll tie you down and you won't be able to sit at your graduation ceremony. If that's not enough to make you behave, there's always the ginger lube."

She whimpered around his cock and one hand came up to cup his balls. Sensation sizzled up his spine. Deena worked to take him inside, finding that perfect rhythm where every second was pure bliss. There wasn't a moment when he couldn't feel the heat of her mouth, the soft pull of her lips.

He tugged at her hair. "Time to take care of you."

She gave his cock one more kiss and then rose to her feet, her nipples brushing against his chest. "You always do."

With a wink, she turned and he caught sight of the prettiest ass he'd ever seen. His cock tightened as she placed her hands flat on either arm of the chair and bent over, her legs wide apart. He couldn't help but remember the first awkward times when they hadn't been in synch. Now they knew their roles. Deena understood what pleasure waited for her so she no longer played bratty games. She simply turned and offered herself to him.

He silently thanked whoever had prepped the room for him. Everything he needed was on a lovely table along the wall. All the toys and fun torture implements he'd bought for Deena were sitting right there like a buffet of delights. Everything he needed to make his sub scream was in his grasp.

He kicked off his boots and shoved out of his leathers. He grabbed a condom, the lube, and a very special toy he'd found just for this occasion. A pretty pink vibrating dildo complete with straps to hold it in place so he could fill his sub up. Everything had been cleaned and was ready for action.

It was time to take what was his.

* * * *

Deena clutched the arms of the chair and decided her Dom really understood what torture was. Waiting. It was killing her, but she suspected Eric knew that. She kept her gaze forward. The very last thing she wanted was to stop all the forward progress they were making so he could indulge his spanky hand.

"You're being a very good girl."

She was a terrifically impatient girl, but that would buy her a sore bottom and no orgasm. "It's a special night for us. I thought you would appreciate a little obedience."

His big palm cupped one of her cheeks, sending a wave of heat through her system. "I always appreciate obedience. Well, unless I need a swift kick in the ass. Did I tell you how much I appreciate what you did for me the other day?"

After their meeting with Mitch, he'd been very appreciative in the cab of his truck. He'd tried to be appreciative in Chef's office, but Big Tag and Charlotte had gotten there first, much to Chef's chagrin. Deena had worked the rest of her shift with a smile on her face.

"You might have mentioned it, Master."

His deep voice seemed to go straight to her feminine center. "You were magnificent and smart and so fucking brave. Did you want to run?"

She could feel him moving behind her. The need to turn and find out what he was doing was almost overwhelming, but she held her ground. "You know I did and you know why I didn't."

"Because you love me."

Something scratchy was laid on her back and she had to keep very still so she didn't lose it. Eric liked to play this game. He turned her back into his sexual prep table. "Because I love you. Because I finally figured out that what we have is worth fighting for. Even if it means I have to fight your own stubbornness."

He chuckled. "Well, my love, you would understand the word. Don't move. I need to get you warmed up."

She expected him to spread her cheeks, but a callused hand moved around her hips, finding her clitoris. The man knew exactly how to touch her. It felt so good she wasn't about to tell him that she was already hot for him. Taking that monster cock of his in her mouth had done the trick. The taste of him lingered on her lips.

He rubbed the pad of his finger over and around, building the sensation while she was forced to remain still or lose whatever he'd placed on her back. What was it? That was all part of the glorious mind fuck. The implement of her torture/pleasure was right there, but she couldn't see it.

This was the fight she had every time they played. Deena was forced to give in, to give over to him. It was all right because she trusted him. She could submit to him in this place because he valued her, needed her to lead in other places. They'd found their beautiful balance.

She breathed in, letting the scent of the candles and her own arousal flow over her. There would be challenges to come, but they would always find refuge here. Not always in this room or this club. They didn't need a specific place. Home was no longer an apartment or a house. It was him. It was them and their life together.

The orgasm built, threatening to sweep over her. That was the moment he withdrew his hand.

She bit back a curse. So close. It had been right there.

"My poor sub," he said, moving his hand to her back. "Don't worry. I'll take you back there, but not yet."

Bastard. She was dying and she could hear him fiddling with something. The weight came off her back and there was the sound of Velcro pulling apart.

What the hell was he doing? She stared straight ahead at the leather of the chair, her heart starting to pound. No idea. There was no grand light bulb going on in her head, but she knew whatever it was, Eric would make it magical. The man had made her like butt plugs. He could work miracles.

"I bought this for you, for tonight. Your gift tomorrow is a little more practical and I doubt we can write this off our taxes."

She'd already seen the laptop he'd gotten for her. It would come in handy with her new job. What was the gift he'd bought for tonight? Something soft went around her waist and he cinched it tight before running the apparatus down one thigh and back around.

"This should keep you occupied while I work my way into your sweet ass."

Her eyes nearly rolled into the back of her head as she felt the first touch of the vibe.

"The straps will hold it in place. It's a very technologically progressive toy." He started to move the vibrator inside her, working it in and pulling it out. He must have flicked it on because she could suddenly hear the sound of it moving and rotating.

She went up on her toes as he pressed it up and then she sank back, allowing the toy to fill her up. The vibe worked inside her, moving all around and lighting her up.

A gasp puffed from her mouth because there was no way she could hold off for very long.

He strapped the vibe in, letting the toy fuck her while he prepped her ass. Her fingers clutched the leather of the chair as she felt cool lube on her warm skin. Hot and cold. Her pussy was so warm, the vibe working to bring her pleasure while she could feel Eric's finger beginning to massage her asshole. The contrast of the two sensations nearly caused her to scream out.

It was too much, but in the best possible way.

"A little more and then you can move," he promised. "Tell me if you don't like this, baby. I don't want you doing anything that doesn't make you happy."

"I like it, Master." He was completely insane if he thought she'd let him plug her for weeks because she was being submissive. "It was weird at first, and now I want it so bad I can't breathe. Please. I want your cock inside me. I want to feel full."

Full of him. His toy. His cock. She wanted everything he had to give her.

Something far larger than his fingers began to breach her ass.

Pressure built from inside and out. The vibe worked its magic, gliding over and up and back again. Fucking her in short passes. All the while, she could feel her Master's cock thrusting and circling and finally gaining ground.

The head of his dick forced its way inside and her breath came in gasping pants.

A jangled, ragged pleasure started to ride over her.

"Do you have any idea how good you feel?" His hands were on her hips, clutching her like she was the only real thing in the world. "So hot and tight and god, I can feel the damn vibrator. Take more. Take more of me. I want you to take all of me."

She took a deep breath and flattened out her back, offering him the best angle possible. His cock felt so different than the plastic plug. Warm, rigid flesh filled her. He forced his way in, the sensation combining with the pleasure of the vibe. Her whole body felt alive, on fire. Every nerve was awake, every muscle pulsing.

He tugged on her hips and she felt the hot length of his cock deep inside. The vibrator slid over and over while he started to pull out.

Deena couldn't stand another moment. She moved, trying to keep him inside, desperate to keep that feeling going. It was more than anything she'd felt before. Hotter, stronger. She could feel his hands on her, his legs against hers. As he dragged his cock out, nerve endings lit up and sparked through her body.

"That's what I want." He pushed back in. "Fight me for it. Come for me."

He set a pounding rhythm, matching the vibe. Between the two, she couldn't hold out. She pressed back and rode the wave. The vibrator slid over her G-spot while Eric moved behind her.

She felt him shudder as her whole body seemed to shake with the force of her pleasure.

He called out her name and a sense of peace swept over her.

This was what she'd waited for, what she'd been missing.

EPILOGUE

Deena hugged her mom as she stepped out of the auditorium where graduation had been held. She'd worried a little that she would be one of the oldest graduates there, but she'd found herself surrounded by people of all ages. It seemed the seeking of a better life wasn't only for the twenty-year-olds of the world.

Sometimes a woman simply had to be ready to find a new way.

"I'm so proud of you." Her mother held her tight.

"I'm proud of you, too." She'd been very surprised to discover that the reason her mom hadn't wanted to stay with her was because she'd brought a date. Deena looked over and saw Eric talking to her mother's new boyfriend. Tiffany, Macon, and Ally were standing there as well, forming a circle as they waited for her. Graham Sinclair was an attractive man in his early sixties. He was a professor who taught philosophy at a local college. They'd met online when her mother had found the courage to move on with her life.

"He's a good man," her mother said, looking over at the group.

"He seems that way. I like him a lot." She'd only met him yesterday morning at breakfast, but he'd been a gentleman with her mother. He'd pulled out the chair for her, made certain she had everything she needed. It was good to see someone putting her mother first.

Her mother smiled. "I was talking about your Eric. He came to my hotel last night and we talked for a while. He wanted me to understand that he's serious about you. Though I suspect if I hadn't

175

given him my blessing, he would have simply tried again."

So that's where he'd gone on his night off. She'd been out with her friends. Eric had shown up to make sure they all got home all right, but he'd let them have fun on their own.

He was a very indulgent Master.

"He's persistent," Deena allowed. "And I'm pretty sure I'm going to marry that man. I'm so happy you found Graham, Mom. I kind of thought you would be alone for the rest of your life."

Her mother sighed as they started to walk toward their men. "I thought so, too, and then I really thought about what happened with you and Eddie. I remember what I said to you at the time. Sweetheart, I was unfair. I was angry and bitter. I'm so sorry about that. When you started college, I realized how strong you were. I wanted to be that way, too. I was selfish to ask you to come home. Sometimes it's easier to stay in the mud than it is to pull yourself out of it. Life taught me that. But you taught me something else, baby girl. You taught me that I can be more. I can be brave. I think I'm going to marry Graham. We'll have to coordinate our schedules."

She never thought she'd hear those words from her mom. Deena hugged her again, her heart full. "I'm so happy for you."

"Hey, let's take this to Top and get some lunch," Eric said, his hand sliding into hers.

She smiled up at him. That was where it was supposed to be.

AUTHOR'S NOTE

I'm often asked by generous readers how they can help get the word out about a book they enjoyed. There are so many ways to help an author you like. Leave a review. If your e-reader allows you to lend a book to a friend, please share it. Go to Goodreads and connect with others. Recommend the books you love because stories are meant to be shared. Thank you so much for reading this book and for supporting all the authors you love!

Sign up for Lexi Blake's newsletter
and be entered to win a $25 gift certificate
to the bookseller of your choice.

Join us for news, fun, and exclusive content
including free short stories.

There's a new contest every month!

SEDUCTION IN SESSION
The Perfect Gentlemen, Book 2
By Shayla Black and Lexi Blake
Coming January 5, 2016

Privileged, wealthy, and wild: they are the Perfect Gentlemen of
Creighton Academy. But the threat of a scandal has one of them
employing his most deceptive—and seductive—talents…

Recruited into the CIA at a young age, Connor Sparks knows
how dirty the world can be. Only when he's with his friends can he
find some peace. So when an anonymous journalist threatens one of
the Perfect Gentlemen, Connor vows to take down the person behind
the computer, by whatever means necessary—even if it means posing
as his target's bodyguard.

Publishing a tabloid revealing Washington's most subversive
scandals has earned Lara Armstrong the ire of the political scene—
and a slew of death threats. To keep herself from ending up a
headline, Lara hires a bodyguard, a man as handsome as he is lethal.

When the bullets start to fly, Lara is surprised to find herself in
Connor's arms. But as they begin to unravel a mystery that just might
bring down the White House, Lara is devastated when she discovers
Connor's true identity—and finds herself at the mercy of forces who
will stop at nothing to advance their deadly agenda.

* * * *

"You're stuck with me for a while. We might as well enjoy the
time, sweetheart."

"What does that mean?" The question came out all breathy and
come-hithery when she'd really meant it as an intellectual question.
Mostly.

"It means follow my lead and we'll get along nicely. Relax,
Lara." Connor's mouth hovered right over hers, and she felt his hands

trail up her shoulders and caress her neck until he cupped her face. "I'll take care of you."

"They'll never buy it." She couldn't quite believe she was standing here with him, her heart threatening to pound out of her chest.

"I'll make them. And I'll make you believe it, too." His mouth descended, covering hers.

Connor was so hard. His lips shouldn't be that soft. But they were, as well as plump and sensual. It had been years since she'd pressed her body to a man's and felt his dizzying heat seep into her cold bones until she melted into him.

His hands sank into her tresses. "So fucking much hair. It's going to make me crazy."

She wasn't sure how her hair could do that, but then he kissed her again and she couldn't think about anything beyond the tingles she felt from having his hands and his mouth on her. He was utterly in control and she didn't care. So much of her sex life up until that moment had been unremarkable. She loved to cuddle, but the actual sex act hadn't thrilled her or even meant much. She'd certainly never just given over to a man. Her high school boyfriends had been too shy, and Tom had never liked kissing much. Lara hadn't minded because he'd been a little sloppy.

There was nothing sloppy about Connor. As he backed her against the cool metal wall of the elevator, he seized her in a slow, thorough melding of lips before he kissed his way over her cheeks, her forehead, and even the tip of her nose, as though he could explore her with his mouth.

"Open to me." His words sizzled along her skin.

The minute she parted her lips the slightest bit, he was on her. His tongue surged in, sliding against hers in a way that made desire spark and her body shiver. Without even thinking about it, she pressed against his until she could feel the masculine part of him thicken against her belly. He didn't do the gentlemanly thing and pull back. No. Connor actually rubbed himself against her as if he couldn't wait to get inside her.

She meant to do the ladylike thing and shove him away . . . except her hands seemed to have the same affliction as her nipples.

180

Before Lara realized it, she'd wrapped his lean waist in her grip. Her left leg slid up his right. He gave a gentle tug on her hair and delved deep inside her mouth, his tongue dominating her.

Somewhere in the back of her mind she felt the elevator stop and heard the ding announcing the fact that they'd reached their destination, but it wasn't until she heard Tom's voice that she came out of her haze of lust.

"Lara? What the hell is going on?"

She finally found the will to push Connor away, to bring her leg—god, it was practically around his hip now since she'd been humping the man's thigh—back down to where it should be. She turned and saw not only Tom wearing a look of pure shock on his face, but Kiki grinning beside him.

"So you hired him after all?" She winked. "Good choice."

FROM SANCTUM WITH LOVE
Master and Mercenaries Book 10
By Lexi Blake
Coming February 23, 2016

Psychologist Kai Ferguson has had his eye on Kori Williamson for a long time. His assistant is everything he's ever wanted in a partner—smart, caring, witty, and a bit of a masochist. More than a little, actually, but that's the problem. Kori won't admit her own desires. She's afraid of him and what he has to offer. Luckily for her, helping patients face their fears is one of his specialties.

Kori knows she wants Kai. Her boss is the most amazing man she's ever met. She's also smart enough to stay away from him. Having been down this road before, she knows it only leads to heartache. She's just found a place where she can belong. Another failed relationship is the last thing she needs. It's better to guard her heart and let Kai think she's frightened of his dark, dominant nature.

When Kai is recruited for an operation with McKay-Taggart, everything is turned upside down. Kai's brother, international superstar Jared Johns, is in town and Kai must juggle his family issues along with a desperate hunt for a serial killer. The investigation throws Kori and Kai together, and they quickly discover the chemistry between them is undeniable. But even if their newfound love can survive his secrets and her lies, it may not be enough to save them both from a killer's twisted obsession.

* * * *

"What are you doing?" Kori asked the minute Jared stepped away.

Yes, that was the question of the hour. He shrugged, trying to make it look like this was no big deal. "I need a sub. Do you have a play partner for the evening?"

He'd been intending to ask Charlotte to find him a sub. He didn't even want to make the decision. He'd known going into tonight that this was an academic exercise. He wasn't going to get what he needed tonight. Another issue he could lay at his brother's doorstep. He certainly wasn't going to relax knowing his brother was watching him. Judging him. So he simply needed a sub who wouldn't mind taking a spanking and answering some questions about it.

Maybe one of the training subs.

That wouldn't work now because he'd seen the way baby brother looked at Kori like he could eat her up and his inner caveman had started grunting and dragging his knuckles on the floor.

"I don't have a partner," she replied, her dark eyes wide. "I haven't had time to find a partner because the minute I walked out into the club your brother found me."

"Well, then you're free to bottom for me." Found her? Yeah, Kai bet Jared had run from the locker room looking for Kori. She was exactly Jared's type. Curvy, pretty, round breasts, and an ass he could grab and hold on to.

He turned to the prep table. He didn't really need to look it over. He'd prepped it himself. He'd used the time to psych himself up to not murder his brother's friends. It was so obvious to him that they were hanging on Jared like parasites, and his brother didn't see it. He never saw things like that, and when Kai tried to point it out to him he got called out for being pessimistic or dragging everyone down.

He'd show Jared dragging someone down. Little asshole didn't know what the phrase meant.

"Kai, I don't think this is a good idea."

He was definitely loosing his mind because Kori's soft words made him angry. It was irrational. He knew it even as the questions floated through his head. Did she think it wasn't a good idea because she wanted Jared? Had she gotten a really good look at the man she'd known at some point and realized she wanted him? Had she already had him and now Jared was back and she wouldn't even look at another man?

Irrational. Emotional. Out of control. He hated it.

"Hey." A soft hand moved over his bicep. "I was only saying that because we've never played before. We've always kept a certain distance between us."

Had they? Maybe a physical distance but now that he thought about it she was the person in the world he talked to the most, relied on more than any other. He fixed breakfast for her because she would eat crap if he didn't. She would show up before work and they would sit together and have a nice breakfast and coffee and talk about what they would do for the day.

He missed her on the weekends. He would sit alone and wonder what she was doing, who was taking care of her.

Why hadn't he played with her? He could tell himself all day long that it was about being a professional, but it was wrong. He knew the truth now.

He was afraid of losing her.

What if she was afraid of him? What if she couldn't handle what he needed? What if they played and she hated it?

He knew she played with other Doms and he also knew she didn't have sex with them. He knew she'd asked some of her Doms to go easy on her.

He went hard.

"I won't hurt you." He would hold back. He wouldn't give her a reason to fear him more than she did. "It's just for Jared's education. I'll go easy and we'll use the stoplight system."

Green meant keep going. Yellow meant the sub needed the Dom to slow down, and red put a stop to the play.

He didn't intend to get her to say red. He could control himself.

Her hand moved over him, stroking him. Somehow he could feel her warmth seeping from her skin to his. "Are you all right? Do you think he's here to hurt you again? He told me he'd slept with your fiancée. Kai, I'm not going to sleep with Jared. I'm not going to walk away from my job to be some Hollywood type's girl on call for a few weeks. That's the furthest thing from my mind, so if you want me to go and find a sub for you, I will. Mia's in the lounge. She's in the training program so this would be like extra credit for her."

She was giving him an out. An easy out at that. She'd seen right through him, gotten to the heart of the issue, and was now kindly allowing him a free pass. He could go firmly into teaching mode and that would help diffuse the situation and nothing would change between them.

"I would rather use you unless you're afraid of me." The words were out of his mouth before he could think to keep the damn thing shut. His inner caveman was super talkative and made bad choices. Well, maybe not bad exactly, but certainly not the most expedient decision.

He waited for her to explain all the ways he frightened her. Since she'd come to Sanctum, she'd played around in what Kai liked to call the shallow end of the pool. She stuck to Doms with a light touch, the friendly ones who winked and never brought their subs to tears. She seemed drawn to suspension play and loved rope bondage, but any impact play he'd seen her participate in had been restrained, light. So she would tell him to go pound sand and they would go back to their nice, safe, comfortable relationship.

Kori's eyes flared. "Afraid? Of you? Do you honestly believe that?"

Maybe she didn't understand what he was talking about. "Scared of my sadistic side. I can be rough on a sub. I would keep this scene very restrained, academic. I would respect your limits and try very hard not to hurt you. This isn't about my needs. It's about teaching Jared, so you're safe."

Her arms crossed over those round breasts of hers. In her corset they were shoved up and on display as though she was presenting them to him. He knew it wasn't true, but it looked as though if she took a deep breath, her nipples might pop out. They would be right there begging him to twist them and turn them a pretty red color before he would soothe them with his lips and tongue.

"You think I'm a wimp. You think I can't handle a spanking."

Something about the way she was standing, the tone of her voice, brought out the Dom in him, and he found himself moving into her space. "I am attempting to respect your limits."

"You have no idea what my limits are, Sir."

ABOUT LEXI BLAKE

Lexi Blake lives in North Texas with her husband, three kids, and the laziest rescue dog in the world. She began writing at a young age, concentrating on plays and journalism. It wasn't until she started writing romance that she found success. She likes to find humor in the strangest places. Lexi believes in happy endings no matter how odd the couple, threesome or foursome may seem. She also writes contemporary Western ménage as Sophie Oak.

Connect with Lexi online:

Facebook: www.facebook.com/authorlexiblake
Twitter: https://twitter.com/authorlexiblake
Website: www.LexiBlake.net

Sign up for Lexi's free newsletter at www.LexiBlake.net

Made in the USA
Middletown, DE
16 November 2015